LOOKING FOR LOVE?

. . . .

WITHDRAWN

Your perfect match is waiting
for you within these pages!

As you read, you'll meet lots of amazing guys,
but only one will steal your heart.

How will you find him? Simply make a choice
at the end of each chapter. Your decisions
will lead you to the guy who's right for you.

So pack your bags, and board the plane that
will take you to a fabulous ski resort in the
mountains—where you are guaranteed
to fall in love on the lifts!

OTHER BOOKS YOU MAY ENJOY

FOLLOW *Your* HEART

love on the lifts

jill santopolo

SPEAK
AN IMPRINT OF PENGUIN GROUP (USA)

SPEAK

Published by the Penguin Group
Penguin Group (USA) LLC
375 Hudson Street
New York, New York 10014

USA * Canada * UK * Ireland * Australia
New Zealand * India * South Africa * China

penguin.com
A Penguin Random House Company

First published in the United States of America by Speak,
an imprint of Penguin Group (USA) LLC, 2015

Library of Congress Cataloging-in-Publication Data is available upon request.

Speak ISBN 978-0-14-751093-8

Printed in the United States of America
13 5 7 9 10 8 6 4 2

YOU sit at the airport gate, your feet resting on your luggage, trying your hardest to ignore your sister Angie. She's on the phone with her boyfriend, Cole, whispering about how much she already misses him, even though they saw each other yesterday at school. Thinking about boys makes you feel a little nauseated. It also makes you want to call Nate Harrison, your very-recently-ex-boyfriend. Or at least text him. But you know that would just be an exercise in disaster. After all, the reason he's your ex-boyfriend is that you found out he spent his whole lunch period kissing a mousey-looking freshman in the school library, between the biology and self-help sections. The whole thing was mortifying. But what's even more mortifying is the fact that you miss him. And listening to Angie chatter to Cole is not helping the situation.

Just about when you think their gushiness might make you throw up on your sheepskin boots, Angie says, "Love you, too," and clicks off her phone.

"Sorry," she says, looking kind of chagrined.

You sigh. "It's okay," you tell her. "I'm glad at least one of us has good taste in boys."

Angie looks at you critically. She reaches out her hand, then tips your chin to the left so it catches the sun streaming through the window.

"I have a plan," she says, releasing your chin. "You need to kiss someone you meet on the ski mountain. You need to fall in love on the lifts."

The very last thing you want to do right now is kiss someone. In fact, you were planning on spending your days skiing with Angie and your nights reading the least-romantic books you could find—murder mysteries, you figured, with lots of death and destruction. You wanted to stay as far away from love and kisses as possible.

"I don't think so," you tell your sister.

She pushes up the sleeves of her sweater—the soft gray one you've been hoping she'll get tired of and give to you at some point this winter—and crosses her legs in the plastic airport chair. "It takes a boy to get over a boy," she tells you. "And you have to get over Nate. He's a jerk. He doesn't deserve you."

You know this is true. You know he's a jerk. And you really would like to get over him. "I don't know," you say.

"I'm your big sister," Angie says, which is technically true, but only by fourteen months, which isn't *that* much bigger. "You should listen to me. I know about things like this. I'm an expert in getting over breakups."

You think back over the last few years and realize that perhaps Angie's right. She's been pretty good at getting past relationship implosions and finding new guys to date.

"Okay," you tell her. "I'll give it a try. How does this work?"

Angie turns in her chair, a huge grin on her face. "It's easy. You just find a boy, flirt, and kiss him. I mean, you *might* fall in love on the lifts, but all you need is a kiss. A kiss to remind you that there are other boys who are out there. Other boys who like you. Deal?" she asks, putting her hand out so you can shake it.

You reach your hand out and shake.

And just as you do, your flight starts boarding—

destination: Galaxy Ski Resort, where your family has rented a chalet for at least one week each winter ever since you were five. Your parents come over from their chairs on the other side of the waiting area, and you board the plane as a group, rolling your suitcases behind you. But instead of thinking about how to stop your bag from twisting on its wheels and banging into your ankles, you're thinking about kisses, and boys, and who you'll meet when you get to the ski mountain.

Continue to page 5.

THE next morning, you and Angie are dressed and ready to hit the slopes. The chalet your parents rented is close enough to the chairlift that you can ski there directly from the front door. Pretty cool, actually. They're still sleeping inside, but you and Angie wanted to get an early start. With only six days of skiing, you didn't want to miss out on any of it.

As you wait for Angie to buckle her boots and click them into her ski bindings, your mind drifts back to the kissing plan.

"Do you really think kissing someone new will help me get over Nate?" you ask.

Angie stands up and pushes off with her ski poles. "Absolutely," she answers as she heads toward the chairlift.

You follow, reveling in the way it feels to stretch

your muscles and glide over the snow. Even though it's cold out, it's still sunny, and you can feel the rays kissing the tip of your nose and the tiny spots of skin that are visible beneath your goggles and above your turquoise neck warmer.

You're enjoying the sun so much that you almost plow headfirst into Angie, who has stopped in the middle of the trail.

"What is it?" you ask her.

"I think I found your first kiss candidate," she says quietly, and then points her head to the left.

There's a guy standing off to the side of the lift line wearing a bright red ski parka and black snow pants. His thick mop of brown hair is rendered invisible when he clips on his silver helmet. Maybe he feels you staring at him, because before he slips his goggles over his eyes, he smiles in your direction, and you think you see him wink.

"Whoa," Angie whispers into her purple turtle fur neck warmer. "He totally just winked at you."

"Are you sure?" you whisper back.

"Positive." Angie bumps your shoulder with hers. "Go, ski with him. He looks like he's by himself. I'll make myself some new friends this morning. And if you need me, call my cell." She taps the front of her jacket with her glove, right where her phone is zipped into the inner lining.

You're tempted—he's really very cute, and you did promise yourself you'd give Angie's getting-over-Nate method a try—but you're not sure. After all, you really like skiing with Angie. And maybe there are other guys who might be better candidates.

Turn to page 8 if you decide to continue skiing with Angie.

- - - - -

Turn to page 13 if you decide to ski up to the boy in the red jacket.

8

YOU look at the guy in the red jacket again, and then back at your sister. You shrug.

"I don't think I'm ready yet," you tell her. "Plus, I want to do at least one run with you. It's our first of the season!"

Angie shakes her head, but says, "Okay. There will be other guys," before taking off for the lift line with you following.

You slide your skis in next to hers and then shuffle forward each time another twosome gets on a chair. You think about how amazing it's going to feel to zoom down the trails, shoulders square with the bottom of the mountain, twisting your hips so they dip right and left as you fly. Angie skis even faster than you do, so she always figures out which trails you're going to take and goes first. You actually prefer that. All you have to do is follow her purple jacket. She leads you around ice patches and down the best path through moguls.

"Ready?" she asks, as the people in front of you load onto their chair.

"Ready," you tell her, and the two of you push off, mirroring each other as you stop at the red line that's visible through the snow and then turn in opposite directions to grab the pole of the chairlift. You slide the overhead bar down over you both, then look at the mountain below you.

"What about him?" Angie points to a guy in yellow who's zipping through a section of moguls.

"Angie!" you say. "You can't even tell how old he is! He could be forty and married. Seriously."

Angie laughs. "Okay, fine. But I still think you should be on the lookout for kissable boys."

"I know," you say. "I will."

You look down again at yellow mogul guy. He's fallen, sprawled across the side of the mountain. From the way he gets back up, you figure he's probably not forty. But still.

The chairlift is about to reach the top of the

mountain, so you slide the bar back up. You and Angie both get off, and she makes a beeline for the huge trail map that's stuck into the side of the mountain.

As you start to follow, you see an out-of-control skier wobble his way off the chairlift, picking up speed as he goes. He's heading straight for the group of people in front of the map—straight for Angie.

"Watch out!" you shout, as you push yourself faster toward the map.

Angie turns, but it's too late. The guy crashes into the mass of people, and they go down in a pile of pinwheeling arms and ski helmets. You ski over and stop next to the group.

Everyone seems to be getting up, and you let out a breath of relief as you sidestep over to Angie to give her a hand.

"You okay?" you ask.

She grabs your hand, and you help pull her up to a standing position.

"I think so," she says, wincing. "Thank goodness I had this helmet on."

Angie wobbles a little as she sidesteps up the little indentation in the mountain she's found herself in.

"Are you sure you're okay?" you ask.

"Actually," Angie says, "let's go down a green. And maybe I'll sit in the lodge for a little. I think I'm just a little shaken up, not really hurt, but it might not be bad to take a break."

You're shocked. Greens are the easiest trails there are. Angie always opts for blacks. Or even double blacks, which freak you out sometimes because of their steepness. She really must be shaken up to want to ski down a green.

You take a trail named Corvus to the base lodge, pop your boots out of your bindings, and head inside. When Angie takes off her goggles, it looks as if there might be a bruise forming where they made contact with her cheeks when she fell. But other than that, she seems okay.

"Want me to get you someone from Ski Patrol?" you ask. "Or water or something?"

"Nah," Angie answers. "I'm fine. Seriously. No need to worry about me, I can take care of myself. Go ski. Have some fun. Find someone to kiss. I'll give you a call if I leave the lodge. For now, I'm just going to relax."

"Are you sure?" You're a little concerned about your sister, but not too concerned. She seems fine.

And she's telling you to go ski. Plus, she has her cell. And can find Ski Patrol if she needs to.

"So sure," she says. "One hundred percent. You should go."

Turn to page 14 if you stay at the lodge with Angie.

- - - - -

Turn to page 19 if you decide she's okay and that you should go ahead and ski without her.

"ARE you really, completely one hundred percent sure?" you ask Angie, keeping your eye on red parka guy.

"More than that," Angie tells you. "Like, three hundred percent sure."

You briefly wonder how Angie's doing in math, but you keep that thought to yourself. Then you give your sister a huge hug and take off after the red parka.

Continue to page 171.

YOU shake your head. "Not going," you tell her. "I'm not skiing again until I know you're completely okay."

Angie looks as if she's going to argue but then changes her mind. "Okay," she says. "Let's sit over by the fire."

You and Angie clomp across the lodge in your ski boots, walking heel-toe, which makes it a little easier. Angie lowers herself onto the couch in front of the black potbellied-stove-type thing that has a fire inside it.

"How about I get us hot chocolate?" you ask.

She nods. "Extra whip on mine, please."

"Deal," you say, heading over toward the concession stand.

Since it's still early in the morning, it's pretty

empty in the lodge. Most people just started skiing and aren't ready for a break yet. In fact, if it were a regular day, you and Angie wouldn't have made it to the lodge for another few hours at least. Right now, you're the only one ordering at the counter. And actually, you don't see anyone around to order from.

"Hello?" you call out. "Anyone here?"

A male voice yells. "Sorry! Be there in a sec!"

You wonder who this voice belongs to, and if it's someone worth flirting with, since you did promise your sister you'd be on the lookout for guys to kiss, after all.

In more than a second—fifteen seconds, to be precise, according to the sport watch you wear when you ski—a guy comes out of the small kitchen and walks over to where you're standing. He's got spiky blond hair and a goggle tan. And he's wearing a Burton sweatshirt with a Galaxy Mountain pin on it that says ORION.

"Sorry about that. May I help you?" he asks.

"Cool name," you say, gesturing toward his pin.

He smiles and you see dimples appear in each of his cheeks. "My parents like constellations," he says. "My sister's Cassiopeia."

"Funny that you got a job here," you tell him.

"You know, since it's called Galaxy Mountain and all the trails are named after constellations."

Orion blushes. "Not really so funny," he says. "My parents did that."

You're not exactly sure what he means. "They named the trails?" you ask.

He nods. "Yeah, they named the trails—they own the place, so they got to choose. They figured it was perfect—eighty-eight trails, eighty-eight constellations. That's why it's called Galaxy Mountain. Orion's one of the double blacks. Cassiopeia's the bunny hill. Cass liked that when she was little, but now she's not quite as thrilled."

You laugh. You also can't quite believe that this guy's parents own the whole mountain. "So how come you're in here instead of out there skiing down the trail that's named after you?" you ask.

"I board," he says, pointing to his sweatshirt. "But I'm in here instead of out there because my dad wants Cass and me to learn the business. Starting the winter I was fourteen, he's rotated me through different jobs so I know what it's like to work all of them. Right now I'm doing a two-week concession stint. So anyway, is there something I can get for you?"

This Orion guy has intrigued you. You've never met someone whose parents own a ski mountain and who is clearly being groomed to take it over when he's older. There are so many questions you want to ask him, but instead you say, "My sister and I would each love a hot chocolate. Hers with extra whip. Mine with a marshmallow."

"No problem," he says. "I'll be right back."

You watch him disappear into the kitchen and wonder if he was so chatty because he was flirty, or just because he was bored. You look around—the lodge is still pretty empty. You look over at Angie, who has unbuckled her boots and is resting her socked feet on a coffee table in front of the couch.

A few minutes later, Orion comes back with two hot chocolates. "That's five dollars," he tells you, resting them on the counter. "And I gave you an extra marshmallow, no charge. Don't tell my dad."

You laugh as he smiles at you. You unzip the little pocket on the inside of your ski jacket and hand him a five. "Thanks," you say.

You step forward to grab the hot chocolate and wobble in your ski boots. Carrying the drinks across the lodge is going to be treacherous. You wouldn't mind some help, but you don't want to ask. Then again, it doesn't seem as if Orion has all that much to do right now . . .

Turn to page 29 if you ask Orion to help you bring the hot chocolates over to Angie in the hope that he'll stay and chat for a while.

- - - - -

Turn to page 33 if you thank him, then take your hot chocolates and go back to your sister yourself.

"ARE you totally, totally sure?" you ask Angie.

"Cross my heart," she says. "I don't want to ruin your day just because some bum who doesn't know how to ski crashed into me. When I feel less shaky, I'll come find you on the slopes."

You look at Angie one more time, trying to search her eyes for any indication that she really wants you to stay but just feels bad about saying it.

"Really," she says. "Go."

You shrug. "Okay," you say. "If you really mean it."

"I really do," she says.

You remind her to call your cell if she needs anything, and then head back out the lodge door to retrieve your skis and poles. You feel slightly bad about leaving her, but you're still excited to ski, even if you won't have Angie's purple jacket to follow down the mountain.

You check out one of the big maps stuck into the snow next to the lodge and decide to take Ursa Major down to Ursa Minor to the Startracks chairlift down there. It's a black to a blue, which shouldn't be too hard to ski on your own.

Pushing off down the mountain, you feel the wind on your cheeks and see the snow spraying in front of your goggles. It snowed all last night, so the mountain is covered in powder. You think of the sign hanging in the house your parents rented that reads **NO FRIENDS ON A POWDER DAY** and laugh. It's true that skiing on powder is way better than skiing on a mountain covered in slush or ice.

Your muscles are getting used to skiing, and your legs feel stronger. You pause for a second where Ursa Major connects to Ursa Minor and a few other trails come together. No one seems to be in your way, so you take off again, flying down the mountain. You reach the bottom and do a hockey stop, spraying snow as you slide sideways. A woman standing near you with her kid looks kind of annoyed, and you shrug an apology. Then you head toward the Startracks lift and see the same guy in the red jacket from before. He's looking at you, and when he notices you looking back, he smiles. You wonder if seeing him again is fate, or if it's just a coincidence that you should ignore. After all, it turns out skiing alone is pretty fun, too—at least for now.

Turn to page 171 if you ski up to him and ask him if he needs a lift partner.

- - - - -

Turn to page 78 if you smile back but decide to ski into the singles section of the lift line.

"I think it would be fun," Charlie says, and smiles.

Fun sounds like, well, fun. And really, you could use that right now. So you say, "Sure."

Charlie puts his goggles back down over his eyes, and you adjust yours.

"Ready to go?" he asks.

"Ready," you say, and you both take off toward Sirius.

He stops at the top of the trail, and you stop next to him.

"So," he says, "are you a first-in-the-line skier, or a bringing-up-the-rear skier?"

When you ski with Angie, you usually follow her, and you like that, being able to watch where she goes. And also stop where she stops. You don't lose her that way.

"Bringing-up-the-rear," you tell Charlie.

"Perfect!" he says. "Because I like leading. Follow me!"

He pushes off, and you wait a few seconds then push off behind him, following his red jacket down the mountain. There's a chairlift pole in the middle of the trail that seems to have blocked the powder, so the spot looks bald. He raises his ski pole to alert you and then goes left, around it. You smile as you follow him. You like that he was thinking about you enough not only to navigate around the bald patch but to warn you that he was about to do it. Definitely a ski gentleman. He'd probably be a good person to follow in a car, too, you decide as you shift your weight to follow him right—the kind of guy who would gesture with his hand out the window in addition to putting on his blinkers way far in advance.

You get to the mogul patch on Sirius and stop for a minute to watch him. Charlie's form is great. You're not bad at moguls, but he's definitely better. You push off and do your best to get down them without getting stuck or falling. You're moving fast and know that you have a huge smile on your face only because you feel the cold air against your teeth.

When you make it to the bottom of the mogul

patch, you look for Charlie's jacket and find him waiting for you off to the side.

"Nice moguling!" he says.

"Thanks. You, too," you tell him. Then you hold up your ski pole. "Ski high-five?" you ask.

He laughs and high-fives the bottom of your pole with his. "When we get to the bottom, I'm going to use my momentum to get up the hill to the Startracks lift. Meet me there?"

You nod. Then he takes off again, and you follow. The bottom half of Sirius is steep, and you have to concentrate on not going too fast and skiing out of control. It looks to you as if Charlie is doing the same. You're actually pretty well-matched skiers, you think, as you glance ahead to check on his red jacket.

You meet him on the line for Startracks and go up the mountain with him again. You ski a few more runs and then when you're sitting on the chairlift, Charlie lifts his goggles up again. "So," he says, "thoughts on a hot chocolate break? I'm getting a little cold and might need some sustenance."

You look at Charlie. You've had a great time skiing with him so far. And it's been nice getting to know him on the chairlift rides between your runs. There's definite potential here for kissing . . . but you're not sure. There may be other guys out there who have even more kissing potential . . .

*Turn to page 34 if you say sure
and follow him into the lodge.*

- - - - -

*Or turn to page 26 if you thank Charlie
for the offer, but tell him you're
going to continue skiing.*

YOU check the trail map and decide you're going to take Canis Major to Canis Minor. The top trail is a black, and the bottom is a blue. Not too easy, but not too hard, either. You roll your shoulders back and take off, trying to keep in mind everything you learned in your final ski lesson of last winter. Swivel at the hips, top of your body square to the mountain ... You idly wonder if you should look into booking a ski lesson for the afternoon. Or maybe even the rest of the morning. Then you remember you're supposed to be looking for boys to potentially kiss.

You try to get out of your own head enough to check out the people around you. A few couples are skiing together. There are a lot of father-kid pairs, and a few mother-kid pairs, too. You see groups of siblings, it looks like, or maybe friends. There are three kind-of-cute guys skiing together, but you decide that approaching a whole big group of them might be a little too intimidating.

As you ski, you scan the mountain for guys on their own. You spot a snowboarder slightly ahead of you flying off a jump on a kind of flat part of the mountain. He has a lightning bolt on his helmet, and superblond, supercurly hair is peeking out at the back and on the sides. He's wearing a cool plaid jacket, too—he's definitely the first real possibility on this trail. You stop on the side of the mountain to watch him. He takes one of his boots out of his snowboard and then slides himself to the top of the jump so he can take it again. He does a trick this time where he grabs the board before landing. You want to clap but realize that clapping with gloves on from so far away wouldn't really do much of anything.

You decide instead to ski over and take the jump yourself. You build up some speed, bend your knees, and go for it. It feels more like flying than anything you've ever experienced, and you can't help yourself from letting out a little whoop. When you land, you decide to give it another go and sidestep up the slight incline next to the jump. The lightning bolt guy comes sliding in next to you and smiles.

Turn to page 40 if you tell him how awesome his jumps were.

- - - - -

Turn to page 155 if you keep on skiing.

"ANY chance I could trouble you for one more thing?" you ask Orion.

"I'm sure it won't be any trouble at all," he answers. "What would you like?"

You lean over the counter and double-check his feet. He's wearing hiking boots. Easy to walk in.

"Any chance you'd be able to help me take these back to my sister? She's over by the fire. And I'm afraid of wobbling in my ski boots." You give him what you hope is a winning smile.

Orion looks around. "Well, I'm not supposed to abandon my post, but since no one else seems to want to order anything right now, sure. Just don't—"

"Tell your dad?" you finish for him.

He laughs. "Have I said that already today?"

You nod. "Only once, though. And don't worry,

I won't say anything. Plus, I don't even know who your dad is."

"Uh-oh, that makes you dangerous!" he says, as he walks around the counter and picks up the two hot chocolates. "You might start chatting with a stranger and mention the lovely concession stand worker who carried your hot chocolates to the couch . . . and it could turn out to be my dad! Hmm, I think I should probably swear you to secrecy. You can't say a word about this to anyone!"

You glance at Orion's face and see a smile playing across his lips. He's joking, good. Or, at least, half joking.

"Absolutely!" you say, holding your hand up with three fingers showing. "Scout's honor!"

Orion stops. "Are you a Girl Scout?" he asks.

You shake your head. "I always wanted to be when I was a kid, but my school didn't give us the option. So I watched movies about it. That's how I learned the salute."

He's completely smiling now. "You're cute," he says. "You know that?"

You can feel yourself blushing and shrug.

"Well, I'm glad you promised on your faux Scout's honor; otherwise I was going to have to ask you to sign your name in blood. Or maybe just the sauce from the chili. That might've been accept-able."

Chili talk doesn't make you blush, so you answer this time. "Do you make the chili? Chili in a bread bowl is my favorite lunch here!"

You've almost reached your sister now—the lodge isn't that big, but you've been walking slowly.

"Are you ready to have your mind blown?" Orion asks.

"Always," you tell him.

"Not only can I make the chili, but I can also make the bread bowls. I did a three-week stint in the prep kitchen when I was fifteen." He stops a few feet from Angie. "Actually, if you're a chili fan, there's going to be a party tonight in the basement of the main lodge. Chili, hot chocolate, probably bread bowls, too. A lot of the younger staff, and then whoever else we decide we want to invite. What do you think?"

You look at Orion. He's definitely cute and definitely interesting, but you don't feel as if you know him that well. Is he inviting you to be his date? Or just to come to a party. You're not sure.

"Please?" he says.

You look at his smile and wonder if perhaps he's worth pursuing further . . .

Turn to page 52 if you agree to go.

- - - - -

Turn to page 153 if you tell him no thanks and continue walking back to Angie.

AS interesting as Orion seems to be, you figure that if he wanted to help you carry the hot chocolates, he would've offered. So you pick them up and slowly, slowly heel-toe your way back to Angie. You hand her hot chocolate over, lick the whipped cream off your thumb, and then sit down next to her with yours.

Continue to page 176.

YOU decide you're not done with Charlie just yet, so you agree to take a break with him at the ski lodge.

Once you get there, you both pop off your skis and lean them—along with your poles—against the wall of the lodge with everyone else's.

"Near the pile of four boulders," Charlie says, almost to himself as he balances his poles a little better.

"Hmm?" you ask him.

He unbuckles his helmet and you can see his thick, dark hair, a little flattened from its morning of being confined. "A memory trick," he tells you. "When I need to make sure I remember the location of something, I say it out loud. For some reason, it makes me less likely to forget."

You unclip your own helmet and start walking toward the lodge. Charlie follows. "I'll have to give that a try," you tell him. "I always forget where cars are parked in parking lots."

"It's nice to see your whole head," Charlie says, apropos of nothing.

You laugh. "Yours, too," you tell him.

He runs his fingers through his hair, unflattening it a little bit. You do the same to yours, hopefully with the same results. One thing you especially like about skiing is that no one expects you to look all made up and perfect while you're doing it. Everyone's got flat hair and a drippy nose and goggle marks on their face. But even with all of that, Charlie still looks pretty hot.

The two of you clomp up the steps to the lodge in your ski boots and walk into a blast of warmth. Charlie pulls his turtle fur off and unzips his jacket. You do the same.

"That one!" Charlie says, pointing. "Quick, let's get it!"

You follow his finger and see two people getting up from a table. The two of you wobble over as fast as your ski boots will let you and plop down.

"Made it!" you say. "Nice table spotting."

Charlie smiles and puts his helmet on the table. "I'm not usually this lucky with lodge tables. You must be my lucky charm."

The line is a little goofy, but you laugh in spite of yourself and decide that Charlie is pretty sweet.

"So," he says, taking his gloves off and sticking them inside his helmet. "May I treat you to a hot chocolate?"

Hot chocolate is one of your favorite things ever, especially with marshmallows, so you say yes. Plus, letting Charlie buy you a hot chocolate could be the first step toward getting a kiss from him—but it doesn't necessarily have to be, you decide. Kiss or no kiss, you're having fun.

"That would be lovely," you tell him. "And I can guard our table and your stuff."

"Perfect," he says, standing up. Then he looks around. "Right next to the napkins," he says out loud.

You can't help but laugh again. "Now you won't lose me," you say.

"I'd never lose you!" he answers. "Saying it out loud is just a habit."

"Well, I promise not to move tables to mess with you," you tell him. Though the minute you say it you wish you hadn't, because it would've been funny to move a table or two over to see what would happen. But then again, maybe that was something to do once you got to know him a little better. He might not appreciate it just a few hours after first meeting you.

You look around the lodge and see that it's pretty busy. It's getting close to the beginning of lunchtime, and you wonder if it would be smart to eat now instead of taking another break in an hour and a half or so . . .

Before too long, Charlie comes back with the hot chocolates balanced in a cardboard tray. He also has a cup of whipped cream and a fourth cup filled with two huge marshmallows. "I forgot to ask if you wanted a naked hot chocolate or one with whipped cream or marshmallows or both."

"Naked hot chocolate?" you ask.

"Of course, like a naked coffee—the kind with nothing in it," he says, as he puts the cups on the table in front of you.

"You totally made that up," you tell him. "No one calls that a naked coffee."

He shrugs. "It makes sense though, right? I think people *should* call that naked coffee. And should call *this* a naked hot chocolate." He pushes one of the cups toward you. "I happen to like mine with whipped cream, though. How about you?"

You take the cup, and say, "That's perfect, because I like mine with marshmallows."

"Absolutely perfect!" he says, and tips the two huge marshmallows into your hot chocolate. Then he spoons the whipped cream into his. "Cheers?" he says, holding up his whipped-creamed cup.

"Cheers," you say, touching your cup to his.

You both take a sip, and when you look back at Charlie, he has a mustache of whipped cream. You're not sure if you should say something, but finally you say, "Um, I think you have whipped cream . . ." and you indicate the space between your lip and nose with your finger.

"Oh, good," he says, "that's just where I wanted it." Then he touches his finger to the whipped cream in his cup and touches it to the tip of his nose. "Here, too," he tells you.

For a moment you wonder if he's actually nuts, but then he laughs and wipes all the whipped cream off with a napkin, and you laugh, too.

"So," he says, "since my friends are lame and bailed on me today, I was thinking about bailing on them tonight and going to that classic film place in town. I'm not totally sure what's playing, but whatever it is, I'm sure it'll be interesting. Any chance you want to join?"

You think it might be nice to see a movie with

Charlie. But you also think that you could end up seeing something kind of boring and wonder if Charlie would want to change his plans and go in the outdoor hot tub with you instead. You've always imagined there would be something really fun and romantic about being in a hot tub while it's snowing out, and this seems like as good a time as any to test that theory. But then again, you're not totally sure how romantically you feel about Charlie. He's fun and funny, but . . . maybe it would be best to turn down his invitation all together. You take another sip of your hot chocolate and make your decision.

Turn to page 59 if you agree to go—you can't wait to see what happens in the dark!

- - - - -

Turn to page 61 if you tell him you'd love to hang out and invite him to meet you at a ski lodge's outdoor hot tub instead.

- - - - -

Turn to page 151 if you decide that you'd rather keep looking for someone even more romantic than Charlie.

YOU smile back at the guy in the lightning bolt helmet and say, "Hey—nice jumping. I liked that one where you grabbed your board."

The two of you have reached the top of the jump and stop moving. "You were watching?" he asks.

"Just for a minute," you tell him. "I was deciding whether or not I wanted to try jumping, too."

"And you decided yes?" He tugs his mitten on a little tighter with his teeth. For some inexplicable reason, you find this sexy.

"I decided yes," you tell him. "And I decided yes again. I liked how it felt to fly."

"That's the best part of boarding," lightning bolt guy says. "You really do feel like you can fly on this thing, if you do it right. Actually, more so than on skis, I think. My name's Ethan, by the way." He sticks out his mitten.

You shake it with your glove and tell him your name. "So you board *and* ski?" you ask.

He nods. "I grew up around here, so basically I was boarding and skiing before I could even walk right. Have you been skiing for a while?"

"Since I was five," you tell him. "My family tries to get to a ski mountain at least a few times each winter. But I've never tried boarding. It seems scary to have your legs stuck together like that."

Ethan slides himself a little closer to you. "It might feel weird at first, but you'd get used to it, I bet, and then you could really fly."

"Maybe I should try that. Maybe tomorrow." You've never really wanted to board before, but the idea of flying . . . you really like that.

"If you do, you should call me. I give lessons sometimes. Not, like, officially, but for people I know. Let me give you my number."

You wonder if this is a slick way for Ethan to get your number in return. Regardless, you think it might be nice to have a snowboarding lesson from him tomorrow, so you say sure. "But I'm a little afraid of taking my phone out on the middle of the slope . . ." you tell him.

"No worries," he says. "I'm on it." And then he unzips a pocket and pulls out a phone that's somehow tethered to his jacket with a waterproof case and a piece of elastic. He pushes the bottom button and then asks what your phone number is.

You tell him, and he gives his phone a voice command to call you. You feel your phone vibrate in your pocket. "It went through," you tell him. "I'm vibrating."

"Oh, are you?" he asks, his eyebrows raised underneath his goggles.

You can't help yourself. You smile at his lame line.

He clicks his phone off and zips it back into its pocket.

"Listen," he says. "Some friends and I are going to an under-twenty-one club tonight in town. You seem under twenty-one. Wait, are you?"

You nod. "Sixteen," you tell him.

He smiles. "Oh! Me, too! So we're going to this under-twenty-one dance thing at a bar in town. You want to come?"

There's something kind of fun and daring and

out there about Ethan, and you have a feeling that he'd be a perfect person to go to a dance club with. But you're not completely sure a dance club is your scene.

"I can call you later, if you're not sure now," Ethan says. "Now that I have your number."

But you've already decided.

Turn to page 63 if you agree to go.

- - - - -

Turn to page 179 if you decide he's not the right guy to kiss and you want to keep skiing.

YOU give up on looking around for a guy to flirt with and instead concentrate on skiing. You ski down Pegasus, which has an awesome jump half-way down the middle, and then go for Hercules, which is basically moguls the whole way down. When you get to the bottom, your legs are a little tired, but you feel fantastic. You take the Milky Way chairlift up by yourself and decide to try a double black. According to the trail map, Dorado is the most difficult run on the mountain, so you decide that's where you're going.

You ski to the top of Dorado and look down. It's pretty steep and more than a little curvy, but you're feeling good. So you take a deep breath and push off. You're picking up speed a lot faster than you expected, and you decide to ski directly across the mountain to slow yourself down. It works a little bit, but you're still moving pretty quickly when you turn to go across the mountain in the other direction. You feel the edge of your right ski carve into the snow, but your left ski slides on a patch of ice, pulling your leg forward with it. You flail your arms to try to keep your balance, but it doesn't help at all and you fall backward into the snow.

Your helmet hits the ground, and as you slide down the mountain, you feel your binding pop and your left ski goes careening down the mountain in front of you. Because it's so steep, it takes a while for you to slow to a stop. When you finally do, your heart is racing and your neck and wrists are icy cold from the snow that crept in around your jacket.

Gingerly, you sit up. Your head feels fine, your back feels fine, all your limbs move, and none of them are in pain. You let out a deep breath. You're not hurt. Just ski-less. Worst-case scenario, you can take your right ski off and walk down the side of the trail until you reach your left one. It's not the very best option, but a possibility. The best option would be Ski Patrol, but you're not sure how often they come by.

As you're trying to formulate a plan, a woman

stops next to you. She looks like she's in her thirties, and she's wearing a white ski jacket and a silver helmet. "Are you okay?" she asks.

"Fine, except that I lost my ski," you tell her, pointing to where your ski stopped about fifty yards below you.

"I'll tell Ski Patrol when I get to the chairlift," she says. "I'd suggest staying put, though. This run is steep and icy and not all that safe in ski boots."

You nod, glad that she has basically figured out your plan for you. "Okay, I'll wait."

"Ski Patrol will get here soon, I'm sure."

"Thanks," you tell her.

She's already pushed off again but she turns her head and yells, "No problem!"

You watch her ski for a little bit until her white jacket blends in with the snow and you can't see her silver helmet anymore.

Then you start thinking about Nate and how annoyed you still are at him for making you look like an idiot in front of the whole school. And how equally annoyed you are at yourself for not figuring things out sooner. But you immediately realize that's not the most productive line of thinking, so instead you imagine your ideal Ski Patrol rescuer.

You decide it would be a guy who looks nothing like Nate. He'd be tall with red hair and blue eyes, even though they'd be covered with his black ski patrol helmet and orange-tinted goggles. He'd be in college, but maybe just a freshman or sophomore. And he'd be single, of course. He might have a pet, too, since Nate didn't like animals. Maybe he'd be the type who watches the Food Network. Especially those chef competition shows, which you love but Nate hated.

You're so busy dreaming of your ideal Ski Patrol guy that you don't notice when the *actual* Ski Patrol guy skis up next to you with a red toboggan behind him.

"Are you okay?" he asks.

His voice startles you out of your reverie.

"Oh, hi!" you say to him, maybe with a bit too much cheer. "I'm fine, except my left ski is about a hundred and fifty feet farther down the mountain that I am."

"I heard," he says to you. "I'm Jake, by the way."

You introduce yourself and thank him for rescuing you.

"All in a day's work," he says, smiling. "Let me help you on the toboggan."

He lifts up his goggles to do so, and when he does, you see blue eyes and red eyebrows. You hold in your gasp. Is it possible that you have actually been rescued by your dream Ski Patrol man?

"Can I ask you a weird question?" you say, as he lifts you up out of the snow pile you've been sitting in. He's incredibly strong.

"How weird?" he asks, his eyes twinkling a little.

"Mmm, maybe medium weird?" you tell him.

"Then I guess you can go for it," he says through a laugh.

As he slips you onto the toboggan, you ask, "Do you happen to have a pet?"

He looks at you funny, and says, "I do, a dog—how come?"

"And are you a freshman or sophomore in college?"

"A junior, actually," he says. "Are you taking a survey? About people in college with pets?"

That was actually a great excuse. "Yes! I am. Because I'm a junior in high school and I love pets and was thinking I might want to take one with me when I go to college."

"In that case," Jake says as he straps you into the toboggan, "I'd actually suggest something a little lower maintenance than a dog. Cats are much easier. Fish, too."

"Good to know," you say.

Jake straightens up. "Are you ready to head down to your ski?"

"Never been readier," you tell him.

Jake takes off with the toboggan behind him and you relax and enjoy the ride. You imagine this would be terrifying if you were actually hurt, but since you're not, it's kind of like going sledding.

About forty-five seconds later, Jake stops next to your ski and inspects it. "Looks like it's fine," Jake said. "You lucked out. The binding's not even broken."

He helps you out of the toboggan and into your ski. His hand on your jacket makes your skin tingle a little. You wonder if he's feeling the same way.

"But I think I should probably ski down with you the rest of the way, just in case," he says, keeping his hand on your shoulder maybe a little longer than he needs to.

"Are you sure?" you ask. "There must be some actually hurt people who need your help on the mountain."

"Totally sure," Jake tells you. "I wouldn't be doing

my job otherwise. Besides, I'd rather rescue you than, you know, a three-hundred-pound man who doesn't know how to ski at all, but insisted on going down a black diamond and ended up breaking his leg. You know, when people get hurt on mountains, it's mostly because they try to ski above their ability level."

You shudder. "That sounds bad," you say.

"Oh, it is," he assures you. "So rescuing you? My lucky day." He smiles again and squeezes your shoulder.

He really *might* be your dream Ski Patrol guy—could you possibly, magically have imagined him into being? "Well, thank you," you say. "But before we ski, I have one more question for you."

"Yes?" he responds. He looks cute even with his face covered in goggles.

"Do you, by any chance, watch the Food Network?"

"*Iron Chef* is my favorite show!" he says. "How did you know that?"

"Just a guess," you tell him. "Okay, let's go now."

The two of you ski down to the bottom of Dorado, which, by the way, is much easier than the top, and when you get to the chairlift, you thank him again for rescuing you.

He says you're welcome, but then looks at you for an extra beat. "Hey," he says, "since you're such an animal fan, would you be interested in meeting my dog, Archibald? You can get some more information for your survey. After a fall like that, you might want a break from skiing anyway. And my shift is almost over."

Turn to page 69 if you totally melt and agree—nothing is cuter than a boy and his dog.

- - - - -

Turn to page 76 if you thank him for saving you, but decide he's not the guy you want to kiss—plus, you don't think you need a break from skiing at all.

YOU say yes to Orion's party invitation and then spend the rest of the day thinking about it. Is it a date? Will he want to kiss you? Will you want to kiss him? Will it be weird to hang out with another guy after Nate?

It's seven o'clock and you're supposed to meet Orion at eight. All the clothes you've packed for vacation are in a pile on your bed.

"I don't know what to wear!" you tell Angie. "I've never been to a chili and hot chocolate party at a ski lodge before!"

Angie has a pack of frozen peas on her cheek, trying to stave off a disastrous black-and-blue mark, but she removes the peas to inspect your clothes.

"Jeans," she says. "Definitely jeans."

You reach into your pile and pick up two pairs. "Straight leg or boot cut?"

Angie surveys your shoes and the rest of your clothes. "Straight leg," she says. "Sheepskin boots. Long tank top. Short sweater. The brown one."

"Okay," you say, grabbing the articles of clothing she named. "Jewelry?"

"Did you bring that long key necklace you have?"

You shake your head.

"Hoop earrings?" she asks.

You rummage through your makeup case and shake your head again. "I only brought the ones in my ears." You touch your ears and feel the gold balls there.

"Hmm," Angie says. "Want to grab my bag over there? I think I have something you can borrow."

You hand Angie her bag, and she pulls out a pair of gold earrings that dangle down a couple of inches. "Try these," she says.

You get dressed in the outfit she picked out and then put the earrings on.

"Perfect," she declares. "Now hair and makeup and you'll be set."

You brush your hair and then blow-dry it a little so it's smooth. Then you curl your eyelashes, and apply blush, eyeliner, mascara, and lip gloss.

"Am I set?" you ask Angie, when you're all finished.

"Definitely set," she tells you. "And I know big sisters are supposed to look out for their little sisters and protect them and all that, but in this case, I think looking out for you actually means reminding you to let loose and have fun. Do whatever you need to do to forget that jerk Nate."

You reach out and hug your sister. "Deal," you tell her.

Then you put on your coat and head to the ski lodge.

Continue to page 156.

BUT sometimes what you prefer doesn't matter. Because Angie's your sister, and you don't want to leave her alone when she's not feeling well on vacation.

"I think I'm done for the day, too," you tell her. "Let's head home."

The two of you pop your skis on one last time to ski down to the chalet your parents rented.

"Movie?" you ask Angie when you get through the door.

"Yeah, let's see what's on." She flops onto the couch and clicks on the television. "*When Harry Met Sally*!" she yells. "It just started!"

"I'll make us some grilled cheeses and popcorn and be right in," you tell her. *When Harry Met Sally* is one of your favorite sister movies. You've watched it a million times, mostly when you were younger and your parents went out for dinner. You and Angie basically have the whole thing memorized.

As you slice the block of cheddar your parents bought last night on the way to the house and heat up the pan you found in the cabinet, you think about Nate and *When Harry Met Sally*. Maybe Nate is your Sheldon or your Joe, and your Harry is somewhere out there waiting for you. And maybe you'll have to trust the universe to drop that Harry into your life when you're ready for him. In the meantime, having grilled cheese and popcorn and watching a movie with your sister seems like a pretty great way to spend an afternoon.

Especially because when you head into the living room with lunch, Angie has her manicure set out and a copy of *Vogue* open next to her.

"So since we're home for the afternoon, I figured we might as well make good use of our time," she says. "I saw this manicure on the plane and dog-eared the page. Think you can copy it?"

You look at the picture. It's like a backward French manicure, where most of the model's nail is light pink, but the little half-moons near her nail bed are black.

"This looks like an expert-level manicure," you

say. "I can't figure out how they get such a perfect edge on the half-moon part."

You and Angie inspect the picture together. "Go to Google?" she asks.

You pull out your phone and Google *How do I do a backward French manicure?*

Information on "Reverse French Manicures" pops up on the screen.

"Got it!" you say.

You click open the link and it talks about using not-too-sticky tape cut in the shape of a *C*, kind of like the same way you'd use painter's tape to get perfect edges when you're painting a room.

"We don't have tape here," you tell Angie, "but maybe Band-Aids will do just as well. And we can cut them with your nail scissors."

Angie ruffles your hair, and you duck out from underneath her. "You're gonna mess it up!" you say, but she throws a pillow at you. "Do you care? It's just me here."

She does have a point. You stick your tongue out at her even though you're not eight anymore. Somehow she manages to bring out your inner eight-year-old, though. "I'm getting Band-Aids," you tell her.

And then while Harry falls in love with Sally

on-screen, you and your sister fall in love with the impressively professional-looking manicures you do for each other.

"We're pretty fantastic," Angie says, admiring both your fingers and her own.

"We are," you say. And you realize that's something that's important to remember. It doesn't always take a boy to make you feel good—sometimes all it takes is your sister.

CONGRATULATIONS!
YOU'VE FOUND YOUR HAPPY ENDING!

CHARLIE seems as if he might be sensing your indecision and taps on his phone.

"Would the invitation be more appealing if I told you the movie was *Casablanca*?" he asks. "And that it's my favorite movie ever?" he adds.

He loves *Casablanca*? This is an interesting development in the Charlie situation. You've never seen *Casablanca*, but you've always wanted to.

You smile at him. "It actually would," you say. "I haven't seen that movie before, but I've heard it's awesome."

"Oh, it is," he assures you. "It's fantastic. But I don't want to say anything more in case I spoil something."

He seems so excited that you can't help but feel excited, too.

"Let's go back to skiing," he says, standing up and stacking your empty hot chocolate cups along with the cups that held the whipped cream and marsh-mallows. "The movie starts at seven tonight, so we should get in as many runs before then as we can!"

Charlie holds out his hand and you take it. He helps you up from your seat, and you wonder if he learned his classy manners from classy movies.

Continue to page 161.

"I'D love to hang out with you tonight," you tell Charlie. "But what would you think of an alternate plan, instead of the movies."

Charlie rubs the stubble on his chin. "I'm intrigued," he says. "What did you have in mind?"

"Well," you say. You feel your ears getting hot and are glad they're covered by your hair. You don't want Charlie to see your ears blush. "I've always had this dream . . ."

Charlie leans forward in his seat. "Yes?" he says.

"Not really a dream," you tell him. "More a . . . well . . . a fantasy."

He raises his eyebrows, and you wonder if you've really said the wrong thing. "I'm in your fantasies already?" he asks.

"I mean, you could be," you tell him, and now

your whole face feels hot. You know you're blushing for sure, but you forge ahead. "I've always wanted to hang out with a guy in an outdoor hot tub while it's snowing. And well, it's been snowing on and off all day. And, um, any chance you're interested?"

You can't believe you actually said all of that, and you can tell Charlie is amused. It looks as if he's biting his lip to keep from laughing.

"I'm absolutely interested," he says. Then he tucks a strand of hair behind your ear. "You know, you're totally adorable."

"Thanks," you say, uncertain how else to answer.

Charlie stands and offers you his hand. "So until then, shall we ski?" he asks.

Now it's your turn to say, "Absolutely."

Continue to page 166.

SAYING yes to Ethan's club invitation led to spending the day with him, alternating between skiing down mountains while he boarded next to you and watching him do tricks on a half-pipe. A friend of his, Ashley, taught you how to do a few tricks on your skis, which made your heart race and your adrenaline pump, kind of like being with Ethan did. There was something magnetic—and a little exhilarating—about him.

"Okay," Ethan says as the sun starts to set on the mountain. "Meet me at the Butter Rum at nine. I promise it'll be even more fun than that half-pipe." He winks at you and takes off.

You make it back to the house your parents have rented and jump into a hot shower to warm yourself up. When you get out, you climb into sweatpants and a sweatshirt and slip your feet into fuzzy slippers. You peek into Angie's room and see that she's asleep under the covers.

"Hey, kiddo," your dad says as he walks in with a bag of groceries. "Good day skiing?"

You nod. "How about you and Mom?"

"Oh, you know us," he said. "We did a few runs in the morning, but then spent the day in town. Almost bought a sculpture of a giant melting Popsicle for the study, but then decided against it."

You laugh, not completely sure if your dad is serious. You wouldn't put it past them to buy one if somehow sculptures of giant melting Popsicles became cool within their circle of friends.

"Anyway, we got four different kinds of cheese and a few bottles of Sauvignon Blanc, because I found a fondue pot in the kitchen this morning. Dinner's going to be fantastic. Just like we're in the Alps."

Your mom comes in carrying the wine and asks about your day, too.

"I met a great snowboarder," you tell her. "And some of his friends. They invited me to a dance party tonight at Butter Rum—an under-twenty-one thing. At nine. Can I go?"

"Oh, Butter Rum! We saw that place in town," your dad says. "It looked nice. Very speakeasy meets ski chalet."

"Is Angie coming with you?" your mom asks.

You shake your head. "She's tired. Napping in her room," you tell them.

"I think it's okay," your dad says. "Just keep your cell phone on. And be back by midnight."

"Eleven thirty," your mom amends.

"Eleven thirty," your dad repeats.

You nod. "Eleven thirty it is."

After dinner you slip into a pair of skinny jeans, a tight black tank top, and a sheer hot-pink sweater. After some cajoling, you get Angie to let you wear her super-high-heeled booties.

"It's all so I can kiss someone!" you tell her. "Love on the lifts and all that, remember?"

She smiles. "I can't wait to tell Cole about this," she says as she hands over the shoes.

Butter Rum isn't far, but your dad insists on dropping you off. "Call if you need a pickup," he says. "Otherwise, I'll be up waiting at eleven thirty."

You nod, and then head inside. You spot Ethan immediately. His blond curls are springing all over the place now that they're not smashed down by his helmet. He looks over as you enter and you raise your hand in a small wave.

"Hey!" he calls from the bar. "Steve, give her a bracelet, on me!"

A guy who you presume is Steve steps forward and snaps a yellow plastic bracelet around your wrist. "Unlimited sodas," he tells you.

"Thanks," you say.

Ethan has made his way over to you. "Glad you made it," he says as he slips an arm around your shoulders. "Ready to dance?"

You feel that magnetic pull and say, "Sure, let's go."

Ethan slides his hand down to your waist and then guides you through the crowd in the front room until you reach a big space in the back that has a flashing disco ball and a DJ and a crowd that seems to be pulsing to the rhythm of the music.

Ethan pulls you into the gyrating throng of people and starts moving to the beat. You don't feel as if you're quite relaxed enough to dance yet, but you slowly start moving with him. He pulls you close with one arm and whispers, "Close your eyes." You do, and somehow you can feel the music more now. Your body is moving with it—and with Ethan's.

You dance like that for a while, and then Ethan grabs your hand. "Come on!" he says. There are so many people that you're glad he's holding on tight. Then you're up on the stage with him, and he yells to the crowd below, "We're going to jump!"

Hands go up, and Ethan tightens his grip on you and whispers. "Better than the half-pipe, I swear."

The two of you leap from the stage and you feel hands and hands and more hands catch you, holding you up and moving you farther from the stage. Ethan's fingers are still interwoven with yours, so you're moving as a unit.

"Isn't this amazing?" you hear him yell.

You look up at the flashing disco lights and feel the music as if it's inside you as you give yourself over to the crowd.

"Yes!" you yell back. "It is!"

As you move from person to person, you wonder if you'll kiss Ethan after this. You're pretty sure you will. Dancing turns so easily into kissing, and he was holding you so close before. But you decide it doesn't even matter. He's already opened your eyes to a world that is nothing like what you've experienced before and has absolutely nothing to do with Nate. Apparently, you didn't need a kiss to move on, just the chance to try something new and wonderful.

CONGRATULATIONS!
YOU'VE FOUND YOUR HAPPY ENDING!

JAKE'S blue eyes sparkle when he smiles at you. You wonder if it's the color that makes them twinkle like that.

"Maybe you're right," you tell him. "Maybe I do need to take it easy for a little. How far is Archibald from here?"

Jake looks at his watch. "About five minutes on the snowmobile," he says. "I live on the resort property—in the apartments they reserve for staff. And my shift is done in about ten minutes. Do you have regular boots in the lodge?"

You look down at your feet and realize that you don't. You skied right out of the house that morning. "Sorry," you say. "My family's staying in one of the chalets on the mountain—the ski-in ski-out ones."

"Okay." He checks his watch again. "How about

you come with me to Ski Patrol headquarters so I can hand in my walkie-talkie and tell them I'm going, then I'll snowmobile you to your house so you get boots, and then you can come meet Archie."

You can tell already that Jake is a planner, and you like that. You wonder if he has anything planned for when you get to his apartment to meet his dog.

"Sounds good to me," you tell him. "Hey, what's your last name?"

"You mean in case I kidnap you?" he asks, smiling.

"Exactly," you answer. "You seem like you might be very dangerous. You know, the Ski Patrol thing and all. Only very dangerous people want to help people who get hurt on ski mountains."

"O'Connor," he says through a laugh.

You follow Jake to the Ski Patrol HQ, and while he's doing whatever Ski Patrol things need to be done, you pull out your cell and text Angie. "Fell on the mtn and met cute ski patrol. Jake O'Connor. Going w. him to meet dog Archibald in staff apts. B home soon. U ok?"

"K," comes shooting back over your phone. "I'm fine. C U later."

"Later," you write back.

When you look up from your phone, Jake is walking back to you. "All ready?" he asks.

"All ready," you tell him.

He picks up your skis and poles right along with his and leads you to a snowmobile. You've never ridden in one of these things before and are a little excited about it.

Jake secures all your gear onto the snowmobile, and you find yourself admiring his profile. You weren't able to see it when he had all his gear on, but it's a nice one. And nothing like Nate's. Then he climbs onto the snowmobile. You bang your ski boots together to get as much ice and snow off as you can, and then climb onto the seat behind him. The seats are only separated by a little bump in the plastic-y material—it's kind of like riding behind someone on a motorcycle.

"There are hand grips next to the seat," he says, "but you can also hold on to me, if that feels more secure."

You don't waste too much timing thinking about it, and wrap your arms around Jake's ski jacket.

He turns and smiles at you before he puts the snowmobile in drive and heads over to the chalets on the side of the mountain.

"That one," you say, pointing, when he gets close to the house you're staying in.

Jake stops the snowmobile. You jump out and so does he. "I got your skis," he says. "You want to go in and get yourself some boots?"

"Okay," you tell him. You open the garage from a panel next to the door and sit down on a little bench inside the garage. You snap open your ski boots and pull your feet out. It feels so good to have them free that you almost moan in pleasure. You slide your feet into the pair of sheepskin boots you left by the door this morning and head back to the front of the garage to find Jake, who has leaned your skis and poles against the rack the house's owners installed in the garage wall.

"Better?" he asks.

"So much," you tell him. "On to Archibald?"

He runs his fingers through his hair, making it stick up a little, which is especially adorable. "On to Archibald," he says.

A few minutes later, you pull up at a small apartment house that has a door on the bottom floor and then stairs and another door on the top floor. "I'm downstairs," Jake tells you. "So Archie can have a doggie door. My roommates work the concession, so they're out for the day."

"Do you like having roommates?" you ask.

"Is this for your survey?" he asks back, smiling.

You shrug. "Just curious. I've never had a roommate before."

"It's nice having people to come home to," he tells you. "But it's also a pain in the butt when someone drinks all the milk and doesn't buy another carton and then you go to have cereal and you pour out a bowl of your favorite Frosted Mini-Wheats and . . . no milk. Very disappointing. And when someone brings home, like, six people to hang out when you still have one final left to take the next morning. But mostly it's nice. It makes me miss my brothers a little less. For your survey, that was one of the hardest parts about going away to college for me. Being away from my brothers."

He pushes the door open, and a snow-covered sheepdog comes bounding across the living room barking as if he has a very important story to tell.

"Archie!" Jake says as the dog jumps up, puts his front paws on Jake's shoulders, and starts licking his face. Jake turns to you. "This monster is Archibald," he says. Archie turns to you and starts licking your face as well. It's slobbery, but it tickles, too, and you start to giggle.

Archie bounces back down onto the floor, barks at Jake, jumps up and licks you again, and then returns to the floor.

"What is it, boy?" Jake asks as Archie repeats the routine for a second time and then barks again at Jake.

You look at the dog, and then you look at Jake, who is bent down and trying to have an earnest discussion with Archie. It's so cute you can barely stand it.

"This might sound crazy," you say, "but could Archie be telling you that you should give me—"

"A kiss?" Jake finishes, standing up next to you.

You shrug.

The minute Jake steps closer, Archie stops barking and walks away, as if to say, "My work here is done."

"I think so," you tell Jake, looking at the blue of his eyes.

"Smart dog," Jake says, locking his eyes on yours.

"Very," you tell him, taking a step closer.

And then Jake's mouth is on yours, and it feels soft and warm and so totally right. Who needs that jerk Nate when you can kiss a beautiful boy who rescues you from snowdrifts and has conversations with animals? You weren't happy when your ski flew off on the mountain, but now you're pretty sure it was fate.

Jake breaks off the kiss to say, "Wow," and then his lips are on yours again, and you wonder if you should text Angie to say that you might not be home so soon after all.

CONGRATULATIONS!
YOU'VE FOUND YOUR HAPPY ENDING!

YOU'RE feeling totally fine, and you don't like the fact that Jake has invited you to his place already—even if it's under the guise of meeting his dog. You actually might like to kiss him, but you feel as if going to his apartment is too much way too soon. So you thank him for saving you and decide to keep skiing. You're about to head over to the chairlift when you see a sign. It reads:

SKI LESSONS
Beginning, Intermediate, Advanced, Expert
Every hour, on the hour

You look at your watch and realize a lesson is about to start in five minutes. You also realize that the instructor standing under the **ADVANCED** sign is by himself. And is all kinds of cute. He has dreadlocks poking out the back of his helmet, and you can tell that beneath his ski clothes, he's got a long, lean, muscular body. Maybe you should take a lesson. Especially after your fall. This might not be a bad idea at all. Then again, it might be nice to have some more time to ski by yourself, too.

Turn to page 135 if you decide to take a ski lesson.

- - - - -

Turn to page 141 if you pass and choose to keep going to the mogul mountain.

YOU jump onto the singles line at the chairlift. Everyone else is in groups of two, so you get to skip the longer line and have a lift to yourself. Honestly, this skiing-alone thing has its perks. You watch the people skiing below you and enjoy the way the sun feels on your nose. The ride is a bit of a long one, so you stick your poles under your legs and relax against the back of the lift, enjoying the quiet. The snow is falling softly, and you feel a bit as if you're in a snow globe.

You see the end of the lift in sight and get ready to unload.

Continue to page 26.

YOU fasten your boots, pull on your turtle fur, zip up your jacket, clip on your helmet, slide down your goggles, and slip on your gloves. Now you're ready to brave the weather. You head outside into a gust of frigid wind and shiver for a second until your body adjusts to the temperature. Then you snap your boots into your skis, grab your poles, and head off to the chairlift.

The first person you see once you get there is that same guy in the red jacket from before, and he's smiling at you. You can't believe it's him again. Is fate telling you talk to him, or are you just being silly? You're not sure.

Turn to page 171 if you ski up to him and ask him if he needs a lift partner.

- - - - -

Turn to page 81 if you smile back, but decide to hightail it over to another chairlift that leads to harder trails.

YOU smile back at him but decide that you've already passed him over once, and you don't want to double back. Today's kiss challenge is all about moving forward, and that's what you're going to do, no matter what.

You ski down the mountain a short way to a smaller chairlift that leads to harder trails, and you decide you're happy with your decision.

Continue to page 78.

YOU go toward the counter and wait in line while you peruse the menu. It has the usual ski lodge food: hamburger, chicken tenders, pizza, cheese fries, nachos, vegetable soup, house salad, grilled cheese, and, your personal favorite, chili in a bread bowl. You get to the front and place your order, adding in a water for hydration and a cookie because why not. The girl behind the counter fills up a tray for you, and you wobble with it over to the cashier and then look around the room for an empty table. The main trouble with skiing—and eating—by yourself is that there's no one to scout tables while you wait for food.

Finally, you spot an empty table in a corner and wobble over to it as quickly as you can. You put down your tray and remove as much outdoor clothing as possible; otherwise, you'll end up feeling like an overstuffed teddy bear when you eat, unable to get your arms to go all the way up or down.

Just as you're taking off your jacket, two boys come toward your table carrying trays. They look kind of the same, but one has a buzz cut and the other has brown hair long enough to curl over the collar of his jacket. It's held back with a green bandanna that blends nicely with his green eyes. Both of their green eyes.

"Hey," the non-bandanna guy says. You look at his tray and see a cheeseburger, fries, Gatorade, and a brownie.

"Would you mind if we joined you?" the bandanna guy says. His tray has vegetable soup, a salad, a bottle of water, and a banana.

The boys are exactly the same height, and when they smile at you, the corners of their eyes crinkle in the exact same way. You figure that they must be identical twins with non-identical haircuts and taste in food. They're both actually pretty cute, but you didn't really mind sitting alone. Twins might be complicated to handle—but then again, they might also present you with two kissing possibilities instead of just one.

Turn to page 100 if you say yes.

- - - - -

*Turn to page 105 if they seem
like too much trouble.*

YOU decide that if you were going to kiss someone, Ravi would be a good person to kiss. But you don't think you're ready. You disengage from the hug.

"Thank you again," you say. "I'm definitely staying off Monoceros for the rest of my trip."

Ravi shrugs. "I don't know," he says. "I bet you could do it."

You shake your head. "I think I'm going to give Serpens a try instead," you say, naming a flatter, curvier trail.

"Sounds like a plan," Ravi says. "I'm going to head back up to Monoceros. It was nice to meet you."

Continue to page 181.

YOU decide that kissing doesn't matter. At least not at the moment.

"Sure," you say. "I'm up for another trip down Taurus."

"Lovely," Laurent says. "Would you like to race? We can be like two corks, flying out of champagne bottles, seeing who lands first."

You smile at Laurent's very proper grammar and his absurd image of the two of you as flying corks. You would never in a million years use a champagne cork to describe a race.

"She can smile!" Laurent says, grinning himself. "I wasn't sure if it was possible."

You try to think over your interactions with Laurent. Had you been especially frown-y? You didn't mean to be.

"Was I upset before?" you ask.

"Maybe you seemed a little sad," he says.

"Maybe I *was* a little sad," you tell him. "Recent ex-boyfriend troubles."

He puts his gloved hand on your forearm, and somehow there's something very comforting about that. "Well, he must have been an idiot."

"Unfortunately, I think you're probably right," you say. Unbidden, the picture of Nate kissing that freshman girl pops into your head. But weirdly, it doesn't make you as upset as it had just yesterday.

"And now?" he asks. "Are you still sad now?"

"Now . . . now I think I'm okay," you answer. "Or at least I will be."

"Time," he says, "heals a lot."

You can tell by the way he says it that he's speaking from personal experience.

"Has time healed you?" you ask.

"Very much so," he says. "Time and life and the universe. The only way to live is by living and the only way to love is by loving, and sometimes things that seem impossible to handle at first end up being perfectly fine. More than fine even."

You put your hand on Laurent's arm this time. "Thank you," you tell him.

What Laurent is saying makes you realize that there's so much more out there. So many more people to meet and so many more things to experience. There's lots to do besides worry about a jerky high school guy who didn't treat you right.

The chairlift slows to a stop, and you and Laurent get off.

"Ready to go?" he asks.

"Never been readier," you tell him.

And the two of you take off like champagne corks. Even if you didn't find someone to kiss, you think that perhaps you discovered something even more important today. And it took making a new, awesome friend to show you that.

CONGRATULATIONS!
YOU'VE FOUND YOUR HAPPY ENDING!

AFTER some careful consideration, you decide you'd rather go off in search of a kissing possibility. There's no guarantee you'll fall in love on the lifts, but you feel like you owe it to yourself to try. Or at least you owe it to Angie.

You go up and down a few different trails so you can work your way over to the gondola lift. You're crammed in with a family—mom, dad, three kids, and a set of grandparents. You wonder if your parents will one day ski with you and your kids if you have some. They used to ski with you and Angie—until she turned thirteen and you turned twelve and you both petitioned them to ski just the two of you.

Once you reach the top of the mountain, you decide to choose the steepest slope there is,

Monoceros. It's not one that you usually ski when you're here, but you and Angie did it once at the end of last season. It was tough, but you'd made it to the bottom.

You ski over to the top of the trail and look down. And swallow hard. You'd forgotten how sheer the drop looked from up here. It seems as if it's perpendicular to the base of the mountain. You take a deep breath. You've done this before; you can do it again. You start slowly and go a few feet, but you feel as if you're going to fall. You hear your heart beating in your ears and feel your palms go sweaty in your gloves. You need Angie. You need someone. You're not going to be able to get down this mountain. You swallow again and try once more, but the panic takes over. You stop, stock-still, your skis sideways so you won't slide. Your heart is racing, and you're starting to feel a little dizzy.

For a moment you consider taking your skis off and walking down the mountain, but, to be honest, that seems as if it might be even more dangerous with such a steep slope, especially wearing ski boots. You remember that ages ago your dad said you could always slide down a mountain on your butt if you got too scared or it got too hard. You haven't used that advice ever, but there's a first time for everything. You consider it and think it might be your best course of action.

But then someone skis up next to you. It's a guy wearing a light blue jacket and charcoal ski pants. His mouth is covered by a black scarf, so all you can see is his nose poking out from under his goggles. Even in your panicked state, you admire his nose. It's kind of regal.

"Are you okay?" he asks.

You take a deep breath. "Actually," you tell him, "I thought I could get down this trail, but I freaked out. It's really steep. And now I'm not sure what to do. I was thinking about taking off my skis and sliding down on my butt."

He says something, but it's muffled.

"What did you say?" you ask.

He pulls his scarf down so you can see his lips— they're extra pink from the cold. "I said that's a long way to go on your butt. But . . . I have an idea. I've been tutoring first graders for a high school community service project, and, well, not that you're a first grader, but . . . can I give something a try? I'm Ravi, by the way."

You introduce yourself and say, "Ravi, I'm willing to give anything a try."

"Great," he says, nodding. "Don't move."

He skis a little so he's maybe ten feet below you and slightly to your left. "Can you ski to me?" he asks.

You're pretty sure you can ski that far, and you do, stopping right next to him. "Okay, great," he says, skiing about twenty feet in front of you this time, a little to your right. "Can you ski to me here?"

You can handle that, too.

He goes down in front of you about fifty feet. "How about here?"

The panic starts again. You shake your head. "Not there," you say. "It's too steep to go that far."

"Okay," he says. "No problem."

He sidesteps up the mountain until he's about thirty feet away from you. "Here?" he asks.

You nod. The distance doesn't look so bad, so you ski to him.

"Great," he says. "We're just going to do that the whole way down."

Slowly, stopping every thirty feet, Ravi gets you moving down the mountain.

"You must be a great tutor," you tell him, as you stop next to him for what must be the tenth time.

He shrugs. "The kids seem to like me," he says. "And I helped a few of them learn to read. Basically the same way I'm helping you ski, putting small groups of letters together into bigger words."

"Do you want to be a teacher?" you ask him.

He nods. "I hope so. A teacher, then a principal, and then maybe someone who can help develop curriculum or work on education policy."

"That's pretty awesome," you tell him. You haven't figured out exactly what you want to do yet, so you're always extra impressed with people who have.

As you move down the mountain, Ravi tells you about the first graders he works with—about Aiden, who loves reading about animals, and Hannah, who only likes books about princesses.

"There weren't a lot in the classroom," he says, "so I wrote her some. Objectively, they're not very good, but she loved them so that's all that matters."

He wrote books about princesses for a little first grader? That's maybe the cutest thing you've ever heard. You wish you could read one of them, and you tell that to Ravi.

He laughs, but you insist.

"I guess I could tell you the story of the princess who wanted a doughnut," he says. "But like I said, objectively they're really not very good."

"I would be honored to hear about the the princess who wanted a doughnut," you say, as you ski to him once more.

So as you ski down the mountain in small bits, Ravi tells you the story.

"One upon a time," he says, and then interrupts himself. "You know, all good stories have to start with 'Once upon a time.'"

You laugh. "Absolutely," you tell him.

He continues.

"So, once upon a time, there was a princess who wanted a doughnut. She imagined the doughnut in her head. It was sugary and sweet and covered with purple frosting and yellow sprinkles."

"Purple frosting?" you ask the next time you and Ravi are next to each other.

"It's Hannah's favorite color," he said. "So anyway, Princess Hannah wanted this doughnut really badly. It's all she thought about, day and night. Her mother, the queen, invited bakers from all over the land to make her daughter the perfect doughnut.

But Princess Hannah rejected them all. 'Not sweet enough!' Hannah said to one. 'Not purple enough!' she said to another. 'Not sprinkly enough!' she said to a third. All of the bakers in the kingdom came, baked, and left, and not one had been able to create the doughnut of Hannah's dreams. 'I don't know what to do!' Hannah said while she was visiting her royal pony. 'My life will not be complete without that doughnut!' The boy who helped take care of the horses overheard her. 'Maybe you should try to make it yourself,' he said. Princess Hannah was shocked. She had never thought of that. But she liked the idea very much. So she went to the royal kitchen and read the royal cookbooks and started making doughnuts. The first ones were terrible. Too salty. So she added sugar. The second ones looked too blue. Then there weren't enough sprinkles. And then they were too big. Then too small. Princess Hannah spent all day and all night in the kitchen for weeks. Until finally she made the doughnut of her dreams. It was sweet and purple and covered in sprinkles. It was perfect. And Princess Hannah knew that it was extra special because she'd made it herself. The end."

You stop next to Ravi and clap your gloves. "That was great," you say. "I bet Hannah loved it."

"She did," he said. "And it helped her to push through when she was having trouble reading. I told her reading a book was just like making the perfect doughnut."

You wonder if he chose that story to tell you because he didn't want you to give up, either. Regardless, it certainly took your mind off the steepness of the slope, and for that you're grateful.

You ski down to meet Ravi once more. "Hey, look," he says. "There's the bottom!"

It's still pretty steep, but there's not much left— maybe about ten feet or so, and then it flattens out.

"I think I can probably ski the rest from here," you tell him. "Meet you at the end?"

He nods. "You go first. I'll follow, just in case you need some help along the way."

You smile and start skiing slowly down the rest of the mountain. You stop after a few feet and turn your head. Ravi's right behind you. He waves his ski pole to say hi. You wave yours back.

It's still slow going, but you make it to the end and relief rushes through you.

Ravi stops next to you, and you can't help it— you throw your arms around him.

"Thank you," you say to Ravi. "I seriously would still be up there if it weren't for you."

"No problem," he answers, smiling down at you.

Your eyes lock with his and, as improbable as it seems, considering what a lame scaredy-cat you've been and considering the fact that he doesn't really know you very much at all, you think he's about to kiss you. You're not completely sure how you feel about that.

Turn to page 98 if you go in for the kiss.

- - - - -

Turn to page 85 if you decide not to.

YOU decide not to think, not to feel, just to do. After all, thinking is what got you into trouble on Monoceros. You lean toward Ravi, and he closes the gap between you, his lips warm against yours. Your hug tightens and he kisses you harder, his teeth scrape lightly along your bottom lip, making you shiver. You wonder if he wants to spend the rest of the day helping you kiss just like he helped you ski. You want to ask him, but you don't want to break off kissing him. So instead you pull him closer. Sometimes it's better not to talk. And this absolutely seems like one of those times.

Maybe Princess Hannah's doughnut metaphor works with boys, too. And maybe you've found your perfect purple doughnut right here on Monoceros.

CONGRATULATIONS!
YOU'VE FOUND YOUR HAPPY ENDING!

YOU decide you have nothing to lose by letting them join you for lunch, so you smile and say, "Sure." Bandanna sits across from you, and Buzz Cut sits next to him.

"I'm Leo," Buzz Cut says, sticking out his hand.

"And I'm his twin brother, Sam," Bandanna says, waiting his turn to shake your hand.

You introduce yourself and notice that both times they've spoken to you so far, Sam has finished Leo's sentence. You wonder if they'll do this all through lunch.

Leo takes a bite of his burger and then wipes his fingers on Sam's napkin.

"Did you just get meat juice on my napkin?" Sam asks. "You *know* how I feel about meat." He turns to you. "I'm vegan."

"I'm not," Leo says, looking at your lunch. "And I guess you're not, either."

"It might be veggie chili," Sam says. "Is it?"

"I think so," you tell him.

He pushes his bandanna back on his head. "Have you read about the way animals are treated before they're slaughtered? My friend gave me *Fast Food Nation*, and now I can't do it. Chicken, cow, pig—anything that comes from them."

"That's why I didn't read the book," Leo says. "I didn't want to know. And besides, I really like how meat tastes."

"But the antibiotics!" Sam says, peeling his banana. "And the living conditions!"

"I don't want to hear about it while I'm eating a burger," Leo says, taking another huge bite.

"One of these days, I'll convert you," Sam says. "I swear I will."

"Never," Leo says, gulping a mouthful of Gatorade.

"Ever?" Sam says back. He looks slightly pained.

You're enjoying being a spectator during this conversation. They seem like they should have their own reality TV show or something.

Leo's eyes twinkle a little. "How about if you

agree to go skydiving with me, then I'll read your stupid book."

Sam pales. "Mom said you can't go until we're eighteen anyway."

Leo shrugs with his mouth full of french fries. "So we wait a year," he says after he swallows. "I can wait."

You're doing your best not to laugh. Truly, they should have a TV show. Or maybe a podcast.

"I think we're being terrible tablemates." Sam turns away from his brother toward me. "So," he says, "would you ever go skydiving?"

To be honest, you've never thought about it before, but you think that, given the right situation, you might. At least, you wouldn't say no right away.

"Maybe," you tell the brothers.

"My brother's an adrenaline junky," Sam tells you as he eats his salad.

"I am," Leo admits, popping another fry into his mouth. "I ski double blacks, I rock climb, I surf—and on our family vacation last year, I bungee jumped. It was the most incredible feeling. The sensation of falling like that, knowing in your head that you're attached to a cord, but it's, like, your body doesn't understand that. It's *fantastic*."

You originally thought Leo was a bit mean to his brother about the whole meat business, but now you think there might be something kind of crazy-wonderful about him.

"And you?" you ask Sam. He shakes his head. "No bungee for me. I spent that same family vacation sketching. Then when we got home, I did some paintings of the waterfalls and the beaches we saw." He pulls a sketchbook out of his pocket. "Sometimes when I'm skiing, I stop and sketch the trees or the snow or the people on the trail. That's why I like the longer flatter ones. The greens and blues mostly."

He pulls a tiny pencil out from the side of the sketchbook and starts drawing quickly. When he's done, he turns the paper toward you.

"Recognize her?" he asks.

You look at the girl he's drawn, the shape of her eyebrows, the curve of her lips. "That's me!" you say.

He does that eye-crinkling smile and nods.

You're pretty impressed. Both these brothers are cool, but in different ways.

Leo takes the last bite of his brownie, and you rip off a final piece of your bread bowl.

"You ready to go, bro?" Leo asks, piling his wrappers and napkins onto the middle of his tray.

"Almost," Sam answers, swallowing the end of his banana. "We don't ski together," he tells you. "But we always meet up for lunch and then leave the lodge together. It's our good-luck tradition. Listen, we didn't ask what kind of trails you like to ski, but if it's blues and greens, you're welcome to join me for the afternoon."

Leo clears his throat. "And if it's double blacks, you're welcome to join me."

You look at both brothers as you stand up with your tray of trash. It could be interesting to spend the afternoon with one of them, but which one? You like to ski blues, greens, *and* double blacks.

Turn to page 107 if you go with Leo.

- - - - -

Turn to page 111 if you go with Sam.

- - - - -

Turn to page 116 if you decide you'd rather not go with either brother—it's too hard to choose!

YOU tell the boys that you're really sorry, but you're saving the table for your sister and cousins, and they leave to find a table somewhere else. You feel a little bit bad about lying, but brothers just seemed like too much to handle at the moment.

You eat your chili, savoring the spice on your tongue, and look around the lodge to see if there are any other boy possibilities. You notice someone over by the fire whose leg is in a cast. He has it propped up on the coffee table on a couch pillow and is reading a book. You stand up slightly to get a better look. From your new angle, you can see that the book is *Harry Potter and the Deathly Hallows* and that the boy looks as if he's about your age and is at least seven flavors of sexy. He has dark ringlets, long eyelashes, and a smattering of freckles on the bridge of his nose. Part of you is intrigued and wonders what happened to him, but the other part thinks maybe you should just get back on the slopes. You didn't come on vacation to sit in the lodge talking to a boy with a broken leg . . . or did you?

Turn to page 118 if you're curious enough to go over and ask.

- - - - -

Turn to page 184 if you decide to head back to the slopes.

YOU look over at Leo. You think that probably he would be the more fun brother to ski with. And also the most likely to kiss you—that whole risk-taking thing.

"Sorry, Sam," you say. "But I'm more into the double blacks."

Then you turn to Leo. "But nothing too steep. I don't mind anything else, but steep scares me."

"That's why it's so much fun!" he says. "But I promise I won't make you ski anything you don't want to ski."

"Deal," you say, and put out your hand. He shakes it.

Meanwhile, Sam is zipping his pencil and sketchbook back into his jacket. "See you when the lifts close," he says to his brother. "And nice to meet you," he says to you.

You and Leo put your gear back on, snap into your skis, and head toward the gondola. It packs about eight people in it and takes you to the very top of the mountain.

You're smooshed against a window with Leo's leg pressed against yours, and you can feel the muscles shift beneath his ski pants. "You're strong," you say. You're not sure why you said it—it just popped out. But he laughs in response.

"I am," he answers. "Rock climbing does that to a person."

You've never rock climbed, never even thought about it, but now that you have, you wonder if you might like it. "What's so great about it?" you ask.

Leo slides his goggles off. "You know the feeling you get," he says, "when you're skiing on a double black, and everything gels and you're flying down the mountain and you feel strong and powerful and like you've overcome Mother Nature? Like you're invincible?"

You do know what he's talking about. You haven't felt that feeling very often, but once in a while . . . yeah. "Mm-hmm," you answer.

"That's what rock climbing feels like. You and your body are beating Mother Nature. Mountains can't stop you—you're stronger than mountains."

"That sounds fantastic," you say. You find yourself staring at his lips as he talks. The way he purses them to say *mountains* is incredibly hot.

"It is," he answers. "It absolutely is."

A couple of moments later the gondola stops, and you pile out with everyone else, grabbing your skis from the side as quickly as possible. You hoist them onto your shoulder along with your poles, and Leo does the same with his gear. Then he looks over at you and reaches his hand out. You grab it and the two of you hold hands as you walk to the area near the trail map, where everyone is snapping into their skis and boards.

"You know," Leo says. "There's one other thing that gives me that same kind of rush. That makes me feel like I'm invincible."

"Really?" you ask, wanting to keep him talking. "What is it?" The *m*'s in "same" and "makes" were just as sexy as "mountain."

"This," he says, as he pulls you closer to him. Your skis slide to the ground as you let your body mold to Leo's. His lips are against yours now, and for a moment they're cold; then they warm up from the heat of yours. Leo's goggles bang against your goggles until he tilts his head slightly, and then you close your eyes and relax into him.

After a while he pulls away slightly. "Invincible?" he asks.

"Invincible," you answer.

You get the feeling that he's not the sort of guy you'll see again after today, but you also get the feeling that you won't really care. You'll have a whole afternoon of feeling invincible. It might not be love on the lifts, but it sure feels wonderful.

CONGRATULATIONS!
YOU'VE FOUND YOUR HAPPY ENDING!

YOU'RE not feeling the daredevil thing at the moment, but you wouldn't mind some company on the slopes this afternoon. Especially if it's company that might lead to kissing.

"Sorry, Leo," you say. "The double blacks might be a bit much for me this afternoon. But Sam, I'd be happy to join you for a run or two."

"No problem," Leo says.

"And we'll have fun," Sam finishes. "Will you keep your eyes out for anything beautiful I should stop to sketch?"

"Sure thing," you tell him.

The two of you get your gear sorted out and head out of the lodge with Leo.

"So I was thinking," Sam says, "we could go up to the top and take Eridanus all the way down."

You nod. Eridanus is the longest, most ramble-y run on the mountain. It probably takes about twenty minutes to ski down. "Sounds good to me."

You and Sam grab your skis and poles and then walk over to the gondola that takes you to the top of the mountain. You put your skis in an outside compartment and then climb in with six other people. You end up sitting across from Sam. He pulls off his gloves and takes his sketchpad and pencil out of his pocket. Since he seems absorbed in his drawing, you look out the window.

The mountain really is gorgeous, with icicles hanging from the trees and snow blanketing everyone and everything. If someone were looking for a place to film a movie about skiing, this place would be perfect, you decide.

You turn to say that to Sam, but his fingers are moving quickly across his paper, so instead you lean over to see what he's drawn. It's you looking out the window, and now he's working on the view beyond. You see how he made your nose strong and your eyelashes long and dark. You wonder if you really look like that, or if he's changing your appearance a little to make the picture better.

"Should I go back to looking out the window?" you ask him.

Sam looks up at you and smiles. "It's okay, you can watch now. I got you already," he says. "But . . . wait . . ."

He takes his finger and smudges it against the pencil lines that made up your hair, softening them a little. "That's better," he says. He looks from you to his drawing. "You're beautiful," he tells you.

The person next to you in the gondola has stopped talking to the person next to her and turns to you. "Does your boyfriend draw you a lot?" she asks. "That's so romantic."

"He's not—" you start to say, but then the gondola stops and everyone rushes to get out and grab their skis and boards from the compartments.

Sam has put his sketchbook and pencil away and is snapping his boots into his ski bindings. You do the same, and the two of you start skiing, slowly, toward Eridanus. Once you hit the trail, you start to speed up, but you realize Sam isn't doing the same, so you slow down until he catches up with you again.

"If I go too fast, I can't tell if there's something I should stop to draw," he tells you.

You've never skied this slowly before. At this rate, it might take half an hour to get down this trail, maybe longer, but you realize you don't mind.

You and Sam ski pretty much next to each other for a while, both of you looking at the edges of the trail, enjoying the scenery. There's something kind of Zen about skiing this way instead of the adrenaline-fueled way you usually do.

You're scanning the tree line when you see an antler. "A deer," you say, "about twenty yards ahead on the left! Come on!"

You speed up, and Sam does, too, this time, probably wanting to catch the deer in his sketchbook before he disappears into the trees. But before you and Sam make it to the deer, you hit a pile of ungroomed powder on the side of the trail and fall. Sam, who's about three seconds behind you, does the same. You look over and see his face right next to yours in the snow. His goggles are slightly askew, and his helmet cockeyed.

"You okay?" you ask.

"Just cold," he answers, adjusting his goggles. "You?"

"Same," you say, lifting your head a little. "My cheek feels like it's been flash frozen."

Sam reaches out his hand and touches your cheek with his glove. "Warmer now?" he asks.

You have a feeling that if you leaned forward and kissed Sam, he'd kiss you right back. But you're not totally sure if you want to be the one to make the first move.

Turn to page 124 if you kiss Sam.

- - - - -

Turn to page 126 if you decide you don't want to be the one to start the kiss.

"ACTUALLY," you say to the brothers, "I like to ski blues, greens, blacks, *and* double blacks, so I think I'm going to head out on my own. But thank you both for the invitations, and for the lunch company."

"Our pleasure," Sam and Leo say in unison, and then smile at each other.

You smile, too, and then wave good-bye as they head out of the lodge.

You're about to start gearing up to head back out to the slopes when you notice someone over by the fire whose leg is in a cast. He has it propped up on the coffee table on a couch pillow and is reading a book. You stand up slightly to get a better look. From your new angle, you can see that the book is *Harry Potter and the Deathly Hallows* and that the boy is about your age and is at least seven flavors of adorable. He has dark ringlets, long eyelashes, and a smattering of freckles on the bridge of his nose. Part of you is intrigued and wonders what happened to him, but the other part thinks maybe you should just get back on the slopes. You didn't come on vacation to sit in the lodge talking to a boy with a broken leg . . . or did you?

Turn to page 118 if you're curious enough to go over and ask.

- - - - -

Turn to page 184 if you decide to head back to the slopes.

YOU decide that you might as well go over and say hello. After all, you're a huge Harry Potter fan. When you were in elementary school, you dressed as Hermione for two Halloweens in a row, and you know every single spell in all seven books and what they're supposed to do.

"Hi," you say, as you stop behind the couch.

Mr. Harry Potter flinches, and his book goes tumbling out of his hands.

"Aresto momentum!" you say, reaching toward it, but your attempt at catching the book is futile because the whole couch is in front of you.

Mr. Harry Potter looks up at you and smiles. "Hi back," he says. "You startled me. I was in the middle of the part where they're in the Ministry of Magic, and I kind of forgot I was in a ski lodge."

He leans down to pick up the book but can't quite manage it because of the way his leg is propped up in front of him.

"I'll get it," you say, walking over and grabbing the book from the floor. "Sorry I surprised you out of the Ministry of Magic."

"No problem," he tells you, taking his book back. "I'm Javier. Care to join me?" He pats the seat cushion next to him on the couch.

"Thanks," you say, as you sit down and introduce yourself. "So what happened to your leg?"

Javier closes his eyes and shakes his head. You can't help but notice how perfectly his eyelashes curl up off of his cheeks.

"The bunny hill happened," he says as he opens his eyes. "My friends and I came up from Texas to learn how to ski. It was our parents' senior year gift to us—this trip. Well, we got here three days ago, and the first morning, first thing, first ski lesson, I fall totally wrong and break my leg. The Ski Patrol had to come and take me to the hospital, then they set my leg, gave me painkillers, the whole thing. My mom wanted to fly up here, but I told her I was fine, that I'd just relax in the lodge. Luckily, I found Harry seven in the gift shop at our hotel yesterday afternoon, or it'd be a long, long vacation."

"Oh, that sucks," you say, fighting the urge to reach out and touch his cast. It's white fiberglass and looks almost as if his leg is wrapped in bandages of snow.

Javier shrugs. "So what about you?"

"Here on a family vacation," you tell him, "but seem to have lost the family."

"You don't like skiing?" he asks.

You shake your head. "No," you say, "I do. I just saw your Harry Potter book and . . ." You let your sentence trail off because you don't exactly know how to finish it.

"Well, you're welcome to read with me," Javier says.

You like that idea. Nate wasn't into books, and you always thought it would be nice to date a guy who was. Or who at least wouldn't mind snuggling up on the couch and reading together every once in a while.

"No book," you tell him. "I mean, I have some back at the house we're staying at, but none with me here."

Javier looks at you and gives you a crooked smile. "We can share?" he says, but the way his voice goes up at the end of the sentence makes it sound more like a question.

"How would we do that?" you ask, genuinely curious. Does he want to read aloud to you? You wouldn't necessarily be opposed to that, but it might be a weird thing to do in a ski lodge.

"We can each read the same two pages, and then when we're both done, move to the next two. My little brother and I read like that all the time. It's basically the only way I can get him to do his homework. You just have to come a little closer to make it work, so we can both see the same pages at the same time."

You love that Javier helps his little brother with his homework. And that he wants to read in tandem with you. You decide to forget skiing for a little while and see what it's like to read with Javier.

"Okay," you tell him. "I'll give it a try . . . but before I get comfortable, do you want anything from the snack bar? Hot cider? Hot chocolate? Anything?"

"How about one of each," he says. "And we can share."

He reaches into his pants for his wallet, but before he can get it you say, "My treat. You're sharing your book with me."

He smiles with both sides of his mouth this time and says, "Okay, but next round's on me."

As you wait in line at the counter, you can't help but compare Javier to Nate, and Javier seems to win in every department: Looks, brains, personality. It makes you wonder what you ever were doing with Nate in the first place.

When you have the drinks balanced on a tray, you head back over to Javier and set the tray down on one side of him. You set yourself down on the other.

"Thank you very much," he says, lifting up the hot chocolate that has a ton of whipped cream on top along with a marshmallow. You weren't sure which he preferred, so you got both.

"You're welcome," you say, watching him take a sip.

When he's done, he hands the cup to you, and you can't help laughing. His nose has a dollop of whipped cream on the end, like he's a white-nosed clown. He looks so ludicrous like that, and seems not to notice at all.

"What is it?" he asks.

But you can't stop laughing long enough to tell him, so you reach over and wipe the whipped cream off his nose. Before you can grab a napkin, Javier grabs your hand. You look up at him and his eyes lock with yours. It feels as if he's cast a spell on you. Then very slowly he lifts your whipped-creamed finger to his mouth and kisses it, licking the cream off his lips right after.

"Mmm," he says, and you blush.

You're not sure if that counts as a kiss as far as Angie is concerned, but as far as you're concerned, Javier kissing the whipped cream on your finger is a million times sexier than kissing Nate ever was.

"Okay," you say, leaning up against Javier. "Let's get back to the Ministry of Magic."

He wraps his arm around you and holds the book where you both can see it. "I think I'm glad I broke my leg," he says.

"I think I'm glad you did, too," you answer. Because even if you didn't find love out on the lifts, it's very possible you found it in the ski lodge.

CONGRATULATIONS!
YOU'VE FOUND YOUR HAPPY ENDING!

"MY lips are cold, too," you tell him.

You're close enough to see his eyes widen behind his goggles. "They are?" he asks.

"Without a doubt," you say. "See?" Then you lean toward him and gently press your lips against his.

"Mmm," he agrees. Then you feel an increase in pressure against your lips and he's really kissing you. You scoot yourself closer, and he wraps his arms around you. The kiss gets deeper and you don't feel the cold anymore. It's as if all of your senses are focused on Sam—the warmth and feel and taste of him.

Too soon, he breaks off the kiss. "That was . . . wow," he says.

"Me, too," you tell him. "Wow."

He stands up on his skis and reaches his hand down to help you up. You grab it, and then, once you're standing, he kisses you again, softly this time.

"I think," he says, between kisses, "that we should take kissing breaks instead of art breaks. And maybe see if the couch by the fire is free when we make it down to the base lodge."

"Deal," you tell him. "First kissing break is at that big tree. Let's go!"

You take off quickly, and Sam matches your speed. Apparently, he's as eager for the next kiss as you are.

And as Sam slides his arms around you in front of the tree, you wonder if Angie was right. Maybe you did find love on the lifts after all.

CONGRATULATIONS!
YOU'VE FOUND YOUR HAPPY ENDING!

YOU wait a moment longer, but Sam doesn't lean in, so you don't, either. The tension you felt in the air diffuses, and it's clear that the two of you are in friend zone now, for whatever reason. He takes his hand off your cheek.

"Ready to keep going?" he asks.

You pull yourself into a sitting position and nod.

He looks over into the woods, and the deer has gone. "Okay, let's see if that deer is farther down the mountain."

The two of you get up and start skiing, keeping an eye out for the deer. But without the flirtiness of earlier, you're not having quite as much fun as you were before. And actually, skiing so slowly is a little boring. You can't take it anymore, so you yell, "Race you!" and take off down Eridanus.

You toss a quick look over your shoulder to make sure he's following. He is, though you realize that if he wasn't, you really wouldn't have cared all that much. You're a much faster skier than Sam, and the race really isn't a race at all. You get to the base lodge at the bottom of the mountain first, but because you're polite, you wait for him. He's only about a minute or two behind you, you figure, so you stab your poles into the ground, lean against them, and watch the skiers coming down off of Eridanus. You love seeing the little girls skiing together—they remind you of you and Angie. You think about Angie briefly and hope she's having an okay day.

You spot Sam coming toward you now, and a guy in a charcoal jacket is close behind him. When Sam stops next to you, the guy stops, too.

"Sam!" he says, as he hockey stops next to him. "I thought that was you! Where's Leo?" He pulls his goggles up onto his helmet. You can't help but notice that he has incredibly bright eyes. So bright they're almost turquoise.

Sam pulls his goggles up, too. "Josh?" he says. "Hey!"

Then he seems to remember that you're there and introduces you to Josh. You can tell that Josh is trying to figure out what the relationship is between you and Sam and where you've come from. So you decide to help him out.

"Nice to meet you," you say to Josh, holding out your gloved hand. "I met Sam and Leo in the lodge for lunch and was looking for some skiing company for the afternoon. Sam offered."

"Not Leo?" Josh asks. "That's unlike him when there's a pretty girl involved."

"He offered, too," you laugh, blushing a little bit at the compliment. "But I wasn't sure about those double blacks."

Josh nods and says, "Yeah, that guy's a little crazy. I was thinking about doing some off-path tubing, so was hoping I'd run into him. Looks like I found the wrong brother."

"You did," Sam says, just as you say, "You mean taking your own tube and making a trail down a mountain yourself?"

You've tubed the regular way before, but never off-path.

Josh nods. "It's really fun, if you're not too risk averse."

You passed on your chance for danger with Leo because he seemed a little *too* crazy, but Josh seems a little more . . . responsible crazy. And you feel like it might be fun to be crazy along with him. Especially after your superboring run with Sam. You just have to decide if you're willing to take the risk.

Turn to page 130 if you decide to join Josh.

- - - - -

Turn to page 180 if you decide to take off on your own.

YOU decide that you only live once and might as well go for it.

"You may have found the wrong brother, but you found the right girl," you say. "I'd love to off-path tube, if you're looking for someone to come along. I've never done it before, though, so you might have to teach me a little."

Josh's eyes light up. "Yeah?" he asks.

"Yeah," you say. "So how does this work?"

"I'm going to head up Eridanus again. Nice to ski with you," Sam says.

You say good-bye to Sam, then look over at Josh. "Okay, come with me," he says. "We'll take the Stargate chair up to Lynx. That's where I stashed the tubes. There's a nice little run through the trees. It'll be good for your first time."

Josh leads you to Stargate, which doesn't have that long a line. The two of you get on in no time. "Okay," he says, "so here's what'll happen. Once we get to the top of Lynx, we'll ski for a few feet, and then there's a turn off to the right. We'll take off our skis, pick up the tubes, and then you just follow me to the bottom of the mountain. Then we can chair-lift up again to get our skis. Sound good?"

You nod. "Absolutely," you say.

Josh nods. "Okay, just make sure you pay attention. I know you've got a helmet on, and the tubes will protect you, but I still don't want you crashing into any trees."

"Me, neither," you tell him. "I don't want me crashing into any trees, either."

He laughs, and the two of you get off the lift. You both pop your ski boots out of the bindings and lean your skis and poles up against a tree. Josh pulls two tubes out from under a tarp that's held in place with rocks.

"Okay, here we go," he says, handing you a tube. It's light blue and has plastic handles on each side. "Do you know how to steer?"

"With your body weight?" you ask. "Leaning to the left and right?"

"Exactly," Josh says. "Now see the path I made? It parallels Lynx for most of the way. We'll end up popping back onto the trail about a foot before it ends. Once that happens, try to stop and get up. I don't want you to get skied into, either."

You laugh and set your tube up behind Josh's. He takes off down the path and you follow, your heart racing. This is one of the more dangerous things you've ever done. You really hope you can get the steering down. Ski Patrol won't be here to save you if you don't. You gauge Josh's speed and make sure yours is about the same. You follow in his tracks, leaning left and right.

The minute you enter the trees, you notice the quiet. All you hear is the scrape of your tube against the snow beneath you. You're staring at Josh and watch him make a wide right around one tree, then left around another.

"How you doing?" Josh shouts back to you, without turning his head.

"Great!" you yell, without taking your eyes off him.

He goes left around a huge tree—one that's probably like ten feet across—and then it's straight the rest of the way down.

"We're almost there!" he yells again. "Get ready to stop!"

You pop out of the trees onto the regular trail, and since the slope flattens out, your tube stops on its own, right next to Josh's.

"What did you think?" Josh asks you.

"That was fantastic," you say. "Seriously fun."

"Want to do it again?" he asks.

You nod.

"Okay," he says. "The trail I made next to Lyra is even better."

You start to get out of your tube. "Wait," he says. "Can we do something else first?"

You sit back into your tube and turn to find that he's slid right next to you. "What do you want to do?" you ask, curious.

"This," he says. And he leans forward and kisses you. The shift in weight gets your tubes sliding a little. You've never kissed anyone while moving before, and it works for a few seconds until Josh's tube tips over onto yours.

Now you're laughing and he's laughing and maybe looking a little embarrassed, too.

"I guess next time I try that I should wait until we're standing up."

"Not a bad idea," you say, smiling as you roll out from under him. "Next time, we'll try to stay vertical."

Then you both get up with your tubes, matching smiles on your faces. It might not be love on the lifts, but it's definitely fun. And that was the whole point of the kissing experiment.

"On to Lyra?" he asks.

"On to Lyra," you affirm.

CONGRATULATIONS!
YOU'VE FOUND YOUR HAPPY ENDING!

AS you're trying to decide, the ski instructor smiles at you, and your decision is made. You ski over and stop right next to him.

"Hi," you say. "So is this the advanced lesson?"

He looks around at the empty snow. "It should be," he says. "But it seems like no one's interested at the moment."

You pull your goggles up onto your helmet. "I might be," you say.

He pulls his goggles up, too, and lifts one of his eyebrows at you. A pretty cool trick. "Have you been evaluated by the mountain?" he asks.

"Last year," you tell him. "I was advanced."

"Hmm. I'm not supposed to take on any lessons without a current official evaluation from the ski school. It's a new policy this year because people kept putting themselves in the wrong level."

This guy seems like he needs to relax a little. Besides, you're the only one there! Who really cares *what* level you're in! It wasn't as if you were going to slow down the rest of the class or anything.

"Oh," you say. "Well, never mind then, I guess." No matter how good a body he seems to have beneath his ski clothes, and no matter how chiseled his cheekbones are and how cute a smile he has, he seems not that interested.

You turn to ski away, but he says, "Wait! I have an idea. Instead of an official lesson, what if I give you an evaluation? It's not like I have a class to teach or anything."

You're not quite certain what to think. "You sure?" you ask.

He smiles again. "I'm sure. Let's go."

He stops briefly to talk to an older man, then skis off. You follow behind.

"Wait!" it's your turn to say this time. "I don't even know your name!"

He stops at the lift area and turns around. "I'm Matthew," he says. "And you?"

You tell him your name, and then slide into the

"lesson" line on the chairlift and jump in front of everyone. "Best perk of being a ski instructor," he says.

Once you're on the chairlift, Matthew lets out a breath and visibly relaxes. "Okay, we made it," he tells you. Now the smile on his face is even bigger.

"Made what?" you ask.

He pulls the chairlift bar down over both of you. "The new head of the ski school is awful. The guy I stopped to talk to. He's the one who started the new policy, and he's on us for everything. The other day he gave me a demerit for having a shirt that hung down below my ski jacket. For real. He said I didn't look professional."

You like this more relaxed version of Matthew. "A shirt hanging below a jacket is unprofessional?" you ask.

"I guess so," Matthew says. "And you're only allowed three demerits before he tosses you off the ski school staff."

"That's terrible!" You can't believe such a jerk is in charge of the ski school.

"You're telling me," Matthew says. "And I really need this job. I'm starting college next year, and I need a car to get there. My older sister gave me her car, and if I work all season, I should be able to afford the year of insurance. So I can't get any more demerits."

"Yikes," you say, wanting to ask a little bit about his older sister. And also a little bit about where he's going to college. But you're not sure how nosy you can be.

"So I'm afraid," he says, "that I'm actually going to have to give you a ski school evaluation."

"Oh!" you say. "No problem. It actually would be good to have one anyway. You know, in case I want to take a lesson tomorrow or the next day or something."

Matthew raises the bar and the two of you get off the chairlift. "Should we get started?" he asks.

You nod, and he gives you some instructions. "Okay," he says. "I'm going to ski down about fifteen yards. I want you to ski to me, making sure to traverse the mountain at least once."

You do what he says, feeling a little self-conscious as you do it. All of a sudden, you want to impress this guy with your skiing.

"Nice form," he says, when you reach him. "Though I could give you some help with how you're holding your arms."

He runs you through a few more exercises involving turning and stopping and slaloming. It's actually a little bit fun, but all the stopping in between each exercise is making you extra cold. The next time you pause, while Matthew is explaining an exercise to you, you pull your right glove off and slide your hand up into your jacket sleeve. You think about the hand warmers in your ski bag back at the chalet and wished you'd thought to stick them in your jacket pocket.

"You cold?" Matthew asks.

You shrug. "A little," you tell him. "But nothing I can't handle."

He looks at you for a second, and then slips off his mittens. He has liners underneath them. "Here," he says. "We're almost done. But in the meantime, I'll trade you."

You hesitate, but then he takes your right glove and slides his hand inside. It's a little small, but not too bad. "Here," he says again.

You take his mitten and put it on. "Oh that's so much warmer," you say.

"Mittens are amazing," he tells you. "Seriously, much warmer. My sister taught me that. She taught me to ski, too."

You're about to ask about his sister again, but before you can he moves on.

"Okay," he says, "only a few more maneuvers, and you'll be officially evaluated. Think you can last ten more minutes?"

"With your mittens on?" you say. "Definitely."

After your very last exercise, which was following behind Matthew as exactly as possible, he tells you that your level is advanced, which you pretty much already knew, and that he's going to make it official in the Galaxy Mountain system.

"Listen," he says, "I have another ten minutes before I have to meet up for a private family lesson. If you want, I can take you to the gear shop and help you pick out some mittens."

The truth is, if you hadn't stopped so many times, your gloves would've been just fine. You don't *really* need a pair of mittens. But there's something intriguing about Matthew, and you think it might be worth going with him to the gear shop just for that.

Turn to page 145 if you agree.

- - - - -

Turn to page 149 if you decide not to.

YOU head over to the chairlift that leads you to Taurus, the run known for its crazy moguls. You end up riding the chair up with an older woman and her younger son, and they pretty much ignore you while they talk about everything the boy learned in his ski lesson yesterday. You tune them out and look up at the sky. It's almost all white now, and snow is beginning to do more than flurry.

You unload at the summit, check the trail map to make sure you know where Taurus is, and then start down the mountain. You make sure to keep your center of balance right over your boots, and hold your poles within your field of vision. You keep your eyes on the path you want to take through the bumps, and go. You're building up speed, but you're doing fine. In fact, you're skiing these moguls faster than you usually do, but you're totally in control. For a second the thought races through your mind that you're the Queen of Moguls, but you squash it quickly, because that's the kind of thinking that can make a person fall. You stay focused and keep your skis in the valleys of the moguls, always tracing the next few feet of your route with your eyes.

Before you know it, there are only a few more moguls to get around, and then you bend your legs, tuck your poles against your body, and zoom straight down the last bit of the mountain. You hockey stop when you get the bottom, spraying snow everywhere and breathing hard. You're about to get moving again when someone stops right next to you. It's a guy in a yellow and gray jacket.

"You're amazing," he says with a slight accent as he lifts up his goggles. His eyes tear from the cold. "I followed your tracks the whole way down."

"Thanks," you say. "I'm not that good though, just had an especially great run."

"I don't know if I believe that," he answers, sliding his goggles back over his eyes.

You can't place his accent. It's maybe a little French, but not quite. "Where are you from?" you ask, before you wonder if that's a rude question.

"Originally Geneva," he says. "But I came here three years ago for high school. Boarding school, but we're on break now."

You nod. "Me, too. I mean, the break part. I don't go to boarding school."

He laughs. "Well, it's very nice to meet you. Are you here with your school?"

He's very chatty for someone who just randomly skied up to you, but he seems nice, so you keep talking. "No," you tell him. "Family trip. How about you?"

"Family trip, too," he says. "But not my family. My boyfriend's family. He's snowboarding down some easy trails with his little sister today, so I'm on my own. He invited me to join them, but—" The guy shrugs. "I'm Laurent, by the way."

"Nice to meet you, Laurent," you say, and introduce yourself.

He pulls his poles out of the snow where he'd stabbed them. "You heading back to the chairlift?"

You nod, because you were, and then just like that, the two of you are skiing together into the doubles line at the lift. "Want to ski Taurus with me again?" he asks.

You would like to ski Taurus again, but you know

that if you go with Laurent, you'll be bailing on Angie's kissing challenge—at least for a while.

Turn to page 86 if you agree.

- - - - -

Turn to page 89 if you decide to keep skiing alone.

"SURE," you say. "Let's head over and check out the mittens."

Matthew gives you a quick smile and heads in the direction of the base lodge. You follow him and catch up as he's popping his skis off and leaning them against the wall of the building. You follow suit, and the two of you head toward the gear shop.

"My sister introduced me to these mittens," he says. "And they're absolutely the best. I never ski in anything else."

"Your sister sounds pretty cool," you say. You've never met a boy who talks so much about his sister.

"She's the best," Matthew tells you. "She's twelve years older, and there are four brothers in between us. They were all pretty tough on me, but she—" He shrugs. "She looked out for me."

So Matthew's the youngest of six. That must be intense. You don't know anyone who has that many siblings.

"What about your parents?" you ask.

"My dad's a merchant mariner, so he's on a boat for two months at a clip, and my mom's a nurse, so she works long hours. Lizzie was in charge a lot."

"And you were totally her favorite," you say.

He shrugs again and smiles a little. "Yeah," he says. "So she taught me to ski. My brothers already knew how and didn't want me to slow them down. She didn't care. When I teach little kids at ski school, I think about the way she taught me."

Your heart melts a little bit when he says that. "I bet she's really proud of you," you say.

Matthew's smile is a little bigger this time. "Yeah," he says. "I think she is."

The two of you have made it to the gear shop, and Matthew opens the door for you. You walk through and he follows, calling out for Georgina, who apparently is the girl behind the counter.

"My new friend here needs a pair of mittens just like mine," he says. "Can you give her my employee discount?"

You turn to him. "Oh, you totally don't have to do that!" you say.

"It's okay," he tells you. "I don't mind. If there's anything else you need, you can use my discount on that, too."

You start to protest, but then change your mind. It doesn't cost him anything to let you use his discount. It's definitely nice though.

"I think I might need ChapStick," Matthew says, picking up a tube. "Do you know if this one will look too red on my lips?"

"It's hard to tell unless you break the seal and open the cap," you answer.

He laughs. "Good point," he says. "Maybe I'll buy it anyway. It's only, like, two dollars with my discount."

"If it looks too red, you can give it to your sister," you suggest.

"Not a bad plan," he answers, and walks over to Georgina with two singles.

You take out your credit card to pay for the mittens. You're pretty sure your parents won't mind. Especially because with Matthew's discount, you're not paying all that much for a really nice pair of mittens.

You sign the receipt, as Matthew unseals his ChapStick.

"Want to test it out for me?" he asks. "Just in case it looks like lipstick when it's on?"

You laugh. "No problem," you tell him. You take

the ChapStick and swipe it across your lips. "What do you think?" you ask.

"Not too red at all," he tells you. "Is it sticky?"

You press your lips together. "Don't think so," you say.

"Hmm," he answers. "That doesn't sound definitive. I think I need to see for myself."

You hand him the ChapStick, but instead of putting it on, he leans over and lightly presses his lips against yours. The kiss is quick and surprising, but also kind of nice. Actually, very nice. His lips are soft and warm, and just as they start feeling good, pressed there against yours, they're gone.

"Not sticky," he says, looking up at you shyly.

And you wonder if this sweet sort of kiss is the kind Angie had in mind when told you to find love on the lifts. According to Matthew, big sisters are right about a lot of things. And you think that perhaps Angie was right about this.

CONGRATULATIONS!
YOU'VE FOUND YOUR HAPPY ENDING!

AS handsome as Matthew is—and as interested as you are in finding out about his relationship with his sister—you just don't get a kissing vibe from him, and according to *your* sister, that's what you're supposed to be looking for today: someone to kiss. So you tell him that you think you'll be okay with your gloves.

"But thank you for the loan," you say, trading his mittens back for your gloves.

"No problem at all," he says. "If you change your mind later, just ask whoever's in the gear shop for the Outdoor Research Alti mittens. And I'll make sure you're in the ski school system by the end of the day."

"Great," you say. "Thanks for all of that."

You wave good-bye and ski off, your brain still wondering slightly about Matthew.

Continue to page 141.

"I think," you say, preparing to lie a little, "that my parents are going to want me home tonight. You know, it's a family vacation and all."

Charlie nods. "I get it," he says.

"But thank you for the offer," you add. "And the hot chocolate."

Charlie rubs the tiny bit of stubble on his chin. "I think I should probably head back out there," he says. "So I can get a bit more skiing in before going back to the guys. Don't want them to have too much fun while I'm not around."

You smile, even though you wonder briefly if you've made the wrong choice. Too late now though. "No, definitely wouldn't want that," you say. "Have fun out there. And with the guys."

"Will do," he says. "Nice to meet you."

You wave good-bye as he leaves and decide that since you're already in the lodge, you might as well grab yourself some lunch.

Continue to page 82.

YOU look over at Angie, who's resting her head on the back of the couch, and decide that you should probably spend the night with her.

"My sister kind of got pummeled on the mountain," you tell Orion. "I think tonight's probably not the best night. But my family loves skiing here. I'll be here for the whole week. Maybe I'll run into you again?"

Orion's shoulders slump almost imperceptibly, but you notice it. "I understand," he says. "But if you change your mind, the invitation stands. And people around here usually know where I am. So if you want to find me later this week, just ask anyone with a name tag on."

"I promise," you tell him.

Then you take the hot chocolates and head to

Angie. You hand her hot chocolate over, lick the whipped cream off your thumb, and then sit down next to her with yours.

Continue to page 176.

UP close, there's something about lightning bolt guy's smile that reminds you a little too much of Nate. Maybe it's the shape of his lips, or the way his bottom teeth show just as much as his top teeth do when he smiles. But whatever it is, you get a bad feeling and decide not to say anything. Instead, you take the jump once more and then ski off.

Continue to page 44.

WHEN you get to the lodge, you head down to the basement room Orion told you about and end up following a few people in who look about your age. Only a couple of lights are on, and there are two guys with guitars standing on a makeshift stage in the corner playing a Beatles cover.

You look around, trying to figure out what to do next when you feel someone touch your elbow. You turn, and Orion is standing there.

"You're here!" he says. He looks genuinely happy to see you, which makes you relax a little.

"I am," you say. "Now where's that hot chocolate you promised me?"

"Right this way," he says, grabbing your hand and weaving you through a bunch of people until you get to a table set up with empty cups and urns filled with hot chocolate.

"May I?" he asks.

"Sure," you say. Orion fills a cup for you and hands you the hot chocolate, steam wafting off the top.

You take a sip and then another. "This is fantastic," you tell him.

"It's my own special recipe," he says. "My dad is thinking about adding it to the menu. Can you guess what's in it?"

You take a third sip. "Something . . . spicy?" you ask.

He nods. Then bends over and whispers in your ear. "Cayenne pepper. But don't tell!"

You make an *X* over your sweater with your finger. "Cross my heart," you say.

The Beatles cover guys start to play a new song. It's kind of slow and ballad-y.

"'The Fool on the Hill!'" Orion says. "I love this song. Want to dance?"

This guy is full of surprises. A snowboarder who invents spicy hot chocolate recipes, whose dad owns a ski mountain, and who likes to slow dance to the

Beatles? But he's definitely interesting. You put your hot chocolate down on the table.

"Sure," you tell him again.

He pulls you close to him. You realize you're the only two people dancing at the party, but he doesn't seem to mind, so you decide not to, either.

Orion says something, and for a moment you think he's talking to you, but when you look at him, you realize that he's singing along with his eyes closed while swaying with you to the music. Something inside your heart softens a little bit, and you decide that he's completely uncategorizable. Every time you think you've maybe figured out what kind of guy he is, he shows you another part of himself.

"You have a beautiful voice," you whisper to him.

He opens his eyes and looks at you. "Thanks," he says with a half grin. "Sometimes I sing with those guys. Come on."

He's laced his fingers with yours and is weaving through the crowd again until you're in front of the stage. "'Blackbird'?" he yells up to the guys.

"Come on up!" says the guy on the left, the one playing the bass guitar.

Orion jumps up onto the stage and takes the mic. Then he starts singing, and his voice on that song is even more beautiful than it was when he was singing into your hair. It somehow sounds pure and clear—like if crystal could be a sound. Or stars. He sings like the stars.

"Take these broken wings and learn to fly," he sings, looking lost in the music.

And you can't help but think of Nate and how he kind of broke you a little bit, but how that didn't mean you couldn't fly tonight, here, with Orion.

When the song ends, you clap and cheer like everyone else, and Orion jumps down from the stage.

"That was really, really . . . stunning," you tell him.

"So are you," he answers.

Then he bends to kiss you, and his mouth tastes of chocolate and spice and his kiss feels like flying, like soaring into the dark black night, guided by twinkling stars. You know it's not love yet, but you think it could be. You certainly found someone wonderful today at Galaxy Mountain.

"Come on, star boy," you say, breaking off the kiss. "Let's get some more of your spicy hot chocolate."

He kisses you one more time before saying, "You got it," and leading you back through the crowd. You smile to yourself. This is the happiest you've felt in a long time. You're already wondering when you'll be able to see him again. And whether you can convince your parents to spend another week at Galaxy Mountain this winter. Orion could definitely be more than a ski trip fling.

CONGRATULATIONS!
YOU'VE FOUND YOUR HAPPY ENDING!

AFTER a day of skiing, during which Charlie shows himself to be the perfect gentleman, he drops you off at the house your parents rented, gives you his cell number, and promises to come back for you in an hour with a car.

You race inside to shower, calling out to see if anyone's home. No one answers, but you find Angie asleep on the couch in the living room, so you stop shouting and run as quietly as possible into the bathroom attached to the bedroom your mom assigned you for the trip. You shower and blow-dry your hair in record time. (You're afraid that without a blow-dry your hair might form icicles when you walk outside into the freezing air.)

Then you throw on a pair of jeans, a cozy blue sweater that somehow manages to be soft and warm and body skimming all at the same time, and a pair of sheepskin boots. You flick some mascara on your eyelashes and run some shimmery gloss on your lips, and you're ready to go. It's a good thing, too, because Charlie should be here in five minutes! You spray some vanilla-scented perfume in a cloud in front of you and then walk through it—a trick your aunt taught you when you were ten and you stayed with her for a week one summer.

As you're layering on your scarf, coat, gloves, and earmuffs, Angie wakes up.

"Hey!" you say to her. "Where are Mom and Dad?"

"Grocery shopping," she tells you. "Where are you going?"

"To see *Casablanca* with the red parka guy, Charlie."

Angie rubs her eyes. "Do you have his cell phone number? And last name?"

You nod. "Charlie Dorman. And I'll text you his number right now."

You pull out your phone to do it, and Angie says, "You should probably text Mom, too. Especially if you won't be home for dinner. Not that she'll really care all that much, but still."

"I don't know about dinner," you tell Angie. But you send your mom a text telling her you made a new friend on the mountain and that you're going to see *Casablanca* with him. Ever since you started high school, Mom has more or less let you do whatever you want as long as she knows where you are.

You get one back from her quickly that says, "Okay. Give Angie his number, and be home by eleven thirty."

Just as you text back "K," the doorbell rings. You go to answer it, and Charlie is standing there looking even better than he did in his ski clothes. He smells like aftershave and soap, and his hair is still damp under his wool hat.

"You came to the door!" you say. "I thought you'd just honk."

"Never!" Charlie says, laughing. "Is that your sister?"

You turn, and Angie is standing in the doorway to the living room. "I am," she says.

"That's Angie," you say. "Angie, this is Charlie."

Charlie crosses the entry hall and holds out his hand to Angie. She shakes it as he says, "It's a pleasure to meet you."

You can tell that Angie is charmed. "You, too,"

she says. "You'd better take good care of my little sister tonight."

"Absolutely," he tells her. Then he holds out his elbow to you and says, "Shall we?"

You give Angie a look before you loop your arm through Charlie's, and she takes that moment to mouth to you: *Kiss him!*

Charlie opens the door for you as you leave the house, and then again when you get in the car. "I got tickets in advance," he says, as he starts the engine.

"You're so prepared!" you say, and he laughs.

You wonder if maybe this is the difference between high school guys and college guys. Or maybe it's just the difference between Nate and Charlie. You look over at Charlie out of the corner of your eye and decide he really is incredibly sexy. His nose is straight with a little tilt up at the end, and his lips are full, kind of pouty. You imagine kissing them. You imagine liking it.

When you get to the movie theater, Charlie insists on treating you to popcorn and a soda. He wanted to get you candy, too, but you told him you'd had your chocolate fix that day already.

The movie theater is the kind where everyone gets big comfy leather chairs, and you and Charlie find two smack in the middle of the theater.

"Best seats in the house!" Charlie says as the two of you sit down.

When the lights go down and the movie starts, you inch your hand closer to Charlie's on the armrest between your seats. A few minutes into the movie, he's holding your hand, and every now and then when you glance over at him, you see him mouthing the words along with the actors. This really is his favorite film, which is maybe the cutest thing about him.

You hold his hand a little tighter, and he looks over at you and smiles. Then Ilsa is on the screen saying, "Kiss me, kiss me as if it's the last time." Charlie whispers the words along with her and then bends over and kisses you. His lips are warm and taste salty, like popcorn. You find yourself leaning toward him and kissing him back just as hard. He runs his fingers through your hair, and you melt inside. You have a feeling this isn't the last movie you and Charlie will see together—because you're pretty sure you've fallen in love on the lifts.

CONGRATULATIONS!
YOU'VE FOUND YOUR HAPPY ENDING!

AFTER skiing all day with Charlie, you're back at the house your parents rented. They went out to get groceries after grilling you on your evening plans. Even though she hadn't met him, Angie vouched for Charlie, and you passed along his last name and cell phone number just in case. Your parents are pretty relaxed about your hanging out with people at home, as long as they know how to reach you and when you'll be back, so after giving you an 11:30 curfew, they told you to have fun and headed out the door.

"I can't believe I suggested this," you say to Angie, after getting out of the shower. Even though you're about to jump into chlorinated water, you felt like you needed to wash the day of skiing sweat off your body.

"I can't believe you packed a bathing suit," Angie

responded, holding up a black one piece with high-cut legs and a low-cut back.

"I *always* pack a bathing suit," you tell her. "You never know when you might need one."

"Disagree," she says. "Tonight being the exception, you usually do know exactly when you're going to need a bathing suit."

You roll your eyes and grab your suit out of her hands.

"So seriously," she says, "you suggested this?"

You nod as you slip the suit on and braid your hair in one long fish tail down your back.

"Impressive," Angie says. "I didn't know you were this ballsy. Nice job, little sis. Is this part of your Plan to Get Over Nate?"

You had so much fun with Charlie today that you forgot about Nate completely. Still, you tell Angie it is, and she nods.

"I completely support all of this," she tells you. "Here, I have some waterproof mascara."

She hands you the tube, and you apply it.

"Beautiful," she says. "You look great. Natural and fun and flirty."

You smile, finish getting dressed, grab a towel

from the house's linen closet, and head to the hot tub at the lodge.

When you get there, Charlie's already inside, the steam billowing up around him melting the snow before it can hit the water.

"Is this how you imagined it?" Charlie asks. "The hot tub in the snow?"

"Exactly," you tell him, as you shed your clothes and slide in next to him in your bathing suit. He has blue swim trunks on, but no shirt, and you're impressed by his muscle definition. Before you can stop yourself, you're reaching out and tracing them. "Do you work out?" you ask, ignoring the thrill that raced through your fingers when you touched him.

"I run," he says. "So yeah. The coach makes us."

"You should thank the coach," you tell him. "Your body is . . ." But then you stop. You don't know what's gotten into you. You're not usually this forward. You should probably rein it in.

Charlie tips your chin up so you're looking him in the eye. "My body's what?" he asks.

His eyes are brown—a deep, rich brown, the color of coffee with only a splash of milk—and the steam from the hot tub makes him look almost ethereal, like he's from another world, a magical one.

"Your body's beautiful," you breathe.

"Yours is, too," he says, moving his hand from your chin to your shoulder. "You're beautiful."

His hand has slipped down under the water and is at your waist. You've never wanted anyone to kiss you as much as you want Charlie to press his lips against yours right now. His touch makes you shiver.

"Are you cold?" he asks.

You're not, but you nod anyway. "Maybe a little," you say.

"Come here, then," he says, pulling you toward him in the hot tub. "I'll keep you warm."

He slides you onto his lap and wraps his arms around you. His mouth is next to your ear. "Better?" he asks.

"Mm-hmm," you say, leaning back against him. All of a sudden, you're incredibly aware of how little clothing you have on—of how little clothing is between your body and Charlie's. It makes you want to kiss him even more.

You turn your head, hoping Charlie will get the message, but he seems lost in his own thoughts while his fingers play with the seam of your bathing suit. You can't take it anymore and turn your head farther so that your body shifts and you're facing him now.

"Kiss me," you whisper. "Please."

Charlie looks surprised for a second and then smiles. "You're amazing," he says. Then he tilts his head forward and slowly, slowly—agonizingly slowly—presses his lips against yours. "Like this?" He breathes the words into your mouth.

You can't take it anymore and slip your tongue into his mouth. Then there's nothing but the hum of the hot tub heater, the quiet of you two kissing, and the soft fall of snow as it settles into drifts on the deck around the hot tub.

Charlie pulls away for a second, his breathing quicker than it had been. "Oh, whoa," he says.

Your breathing has sped up, too. "Yeah," you say. "Whoa."

And as Charlie kisses you again, you can't help but wonder if both of you fell in love that day on the lifts. And when you'll get to see him again.

CONGRATULATIONS!
YOU'VE FOUND YOUR HAPPY ENDING!

AS you're building up speed for the slight incline you have to ski up before you can make it to the lift line, you worry about what you're going to say to him. But before you can figure out a plan, he speaks to you first.

"Hey," red parka guy says. You can't see his mouth under his gray neck warmer, but it sounds a little like he's smiling.

"Hey," you answer back, sliding in next to him. And then it's as if your mouth takes over without passing the words by your brain first. But your mouth is actually kind of smart all by itself. "Is this your first run of the day?"

"Second," he answers. "You?"

You turn. "First. My sister was going to ski with me, but, well, she decided we should meet new people to ski with. You're my first new person."

"I'm honored!" he answers, jabbing his pole into the snow. Then he puts out his gloved hand. "Charlie," he says. "Charlie Dorman."

You introduce yourself as you shake his glove with yours. Then you notice the chairlift line is moving forward, and you shuffle your skis forward.

"You know," Charlie says. "I'm glad you came along. Some guys and I are renting a house here, but it turns out none of them actually wants to ski. I was prepared for a lonely day on the slopes."

You smile inside your turtle fur as you shuffle forward again. "Why did they come if they don't want to ski?" you ask.

Charlie brings his shoulders up so they almost touch the bottom of his helmet in an exaggerated shrug. "Dunno," he says. "I actually don't know these guys that well. We're college freshmen and all live on the same floor, and . . ." He shrugs again.

You shuffle forward again and inch a little closer to Charlie. "Well, their loss is my gain," you tell him.

The people in front of you have gotten on their chair, and now it's your turn. You head to the smooth patch right behind the red line to wait, and you can tell from the way Charlie moves on his skis that he's a good skier. He seems totally balanced and comfortable. Even though you're a little embarrassed to admit it, this kind of turns you on.

The chair comes, and you both sit down at the same time. Charlie reaches above you and pulls the bar over both of your heads. This is usually your job, when you ski with Angie, but you don't mind that Charlie has done it.

"Are you in college, too?" he asks, once you're both settled in the chair, with your poles across your laps.

You shake your head. "High school junior," you tell him.

"Oh!" he says. "You seemed older."

You're not exactly sure what that means, or if that's going to hamper Charlie's kissing potential, but it's a fact, and you didn't want to lie about your age. It wasn't a rule in your deal with Angie or anything, but you figure it wouldn't be right to get a kiss under false pretenses. Like, it would be bad kissing karma or something.

"It's the goggles," you tell him.

For a minute he doesn't say anything, and you worry that you're going to have to explain that you were joking, which takes all the funniness out of it, but then something clicks and he starts to laugh. Like, not just chuckle, but really laugh.

"It wasn't *that* funny!" you say. But now you're laughing, too.

"Goggles!" he gasps, and pulls his own goggles up so he can wipe the tears that have dripped out of his eyes.

His eyes are brown, and when he turns toward you, you can see flecks of gold in them.

"I think goggles do make a person look older," he says. "There's something, you know, mature about the goggled look. It's why raccoons look so mature. Natural goggles."

"Absolutely," you say, as you laugh. "But they don't hold a candle to tuxedo cats. They've won for most mature-looking animal for the last hundred years running. Or so I heard."

Charlie laughs so hard he snorts a little, and then covers his nose, making you laugh harder.

The two of you are cracking up—the kind of laughing where every time you stop, you start up again a few seconds later.

Until Charlie's face changes and he stops laughing completely.

"We have to get off!" he says, looking alarmed.

You look forward, too, and realize that you're

about five seconds away from the top of the lift. Charlie flings the bar up over your heads, just in time for you to get your feet into position to ski off the chair, your poles still in both hands, across your waist.

When you reach the trail map, Charlie is right next to you.

"Whoa," he says. "That was close."

"But we made it," you answer.

"That's a great way to look at it," he says, adjusting his neck warmer. "We made it. So, do you want to ski down together? I was thinking about taking this black." He points to Sirius, one of the harder trails on the mountain. One with a patch of moguls in the middle. You can totally handle it, but you're not sure if you want to. You definitely had fun with him on the lift, laughing like a lunatic, but maybe you're not really ready to kiss someone so soon after Nate. Maybe you need to ski by yourself first. You're not totally sure.

Turn to page 22 if you agree to be Charlie's ski buddy for the day.

- - - - -

Turn to page 26 if you'd rather ski by yourself for the moment.

"HOW does my face look?" Angie asks, turning toward you. "My cheekbones hurt when I touch them."

You inspect Angie's face. There are definitely bruises forming along her cheekbones, where her goggles were pressed into her face.

"Honestly?" you ask.

She nods.

"Honestly, it looks like you're going to have black-and-blue marks on your cheekbones."

"Ugh," Angie says. "Really?"

"Really," you tell her, sipping your hot chocolate.

"I hate that out-of-control skier. Like, absolutely hate him." Angie touches her cheekbones tentatively and winces.

"Me, too," you tell her, and lean back next to her on the couch.

"He ruined our trip," she says, sounding sad and pathetic.

"Not our whole trip," you say. "Just maybe today."

"And my face!" Angie moans. "He ruined today and my face! And if it still hurts to put goggles on tomorrow, he'll have ruined tomorrow, too."

"Oh, Ange," you say, leaning your head on her shoulder. "If it still hurts tomorrow, we can go to the ski shop and get you some sport sunglasses instead. I won't let him ruin this trip for you. Promise."

"But he'll still have ruined my face," she mutters.

You and Angie sip your hot chocolate in silence for a while. You're trying to think of something to say to make Angie feel better when she turns to you and says, "I think I should go back to the ski house. Maybe spend the day watching movies or reading or something. It'll be too sad to sit here and not ski."

"What about if we get the sunglasses today?" you suggest. "Then maybe skiing won't be a problem at all."

"But I'll have a black-and-blue face!" Angie moans. "I think I just want to go back to our chalet."

You sigh, ready to give up your day of skiing, too.

"Okay," you tell her. "Let's finish our hot chocolates, and then we can go."

Angie looks at you. "You don't have to come. You

should stay and ski. Fall in love on the lifts. Seriously."

You're not sure if Angie is offering this because she feels as if she has to, or if she's offering it because she really means it.

"It's okay," you tell her. "I can ski tomorrow. And the next day. And the day after that. We have a lot more days of vacation left."

Angie shakes her head. "You shouldn't give up today, though. I mean it."

You chew your bottom lip, trying to decide what to do. You don't want to bail on your sister if she needs you, but if she really is going to go home to read a book and doesn't mind if you keep skiing . . . well, you'd prefer to be on the slopes. Though also, you're getting a little hungry. So many choices!

Turn to page 55 if you decide to go home with her anyway.

- - - - -

Turn to page 183 if you head back out to the slopes.

- - - - -

Turn to page 82 if you say goodbye to Angie, but stay at the lodge and decide to have lunch.

"THANK you so much for the invite," you say. "But I promised my sister I'd hang out with her tonight. I'll call you about the lesson, though. I still might be interested in that."

Ethan nods. "Sounds like a plan to me. I'll look forward to hearing from you."

You smile and take off skiing.

Continue to page 44.

YOU look at Josh. He seems sweet. And you'd probably have fun hanging out with him. But also, you realize, you'd have fun hanging out by yourself.

"Thanks for the offer," you say. "But I think there are some moguls with my name on them."

"Can't disappoint those moguls," Josh answers.

You smile. If you were in a different place, maybe you'd like flirting with him, but sometimes dealing with boys—and with the emotional ups and downs that come with them—isn't really all that fun.

"I'm going to look for that deer again," Sam says. "Maybe I can catch him this time."

"Good luck," you tell him.

"Have fun," he says. "Nice to meet you."

Continue to page 181.

"YOU, too," you say as you ski off. You've met some great guys today but just didn't feel like kissing any of them. Maybe you're not over Nate yet. Maybe it'll take some time.

But you decide you're kind of okay with that. And you decide, too, that you don't regret being with Nate. Even if he was a grade-A jerk who cheated on you with an unfortunate-looking freshman, now you know what you're *not* looking for in a boyfriend. So Nate did you a favor, really, because you'll know what to look for when you're ready to start dating again.

And Angie was wrong—you don't need a kiss to tell you that your romantic future is wide open. You know in your heart that one day the right guy will be there to lift you off your feet. And when that day comes, you'll be ready.

CONGRATULATIONS!
YOU'VE FOUND YOUR HAPPY ENDING!

"OKAY," you say to Angie. "If you really mean it, I'll head back out there."

"I absolutely do," Angie says. "Plus, you need to find someone to kiss, and you won't be able to do that if you go home with me." She quirks her eyebrow at you, and you laugh.

"Understood," you say with a smile. "But call me if you need me, and I'll ski right back home."

"Will do," Angie tells you, relaxing against the couch. "I'm going to stay here for a few more minutes and call Cole, then I'll head back. Now get out of here!"

"I'm gone," you say.

Continue to page 79.

YOU look at the cover of Harry 7, and then look out the window at the mountains and all the people skiing and snowboarding down them.

Even though you have a T-shirt at home that says DUMBLEDORE IS MY HOMEBOY and have used every sorting hat on the Internet to find out whether or not you'd end up in Gryffindor if you'd been invited to attend Hogwarts, you decide that you can talk about Harry Potter anytime, but you can't ski just anywhere. Since you're on a ski mountain—your very favorite ski mountain, at that—you decide to let the Harry Potter guy enjoy his book alone, and you head out of the lodge to the slopes.

Continue to page 79.

ACKNOWLEDGMENTS

A million thank-yous to all of the Penguins who had a hand in the creation, marketing and sales of this book, especially the fantastic editorial team of Eileen Kreit, Jen Bonnell, and Dana Bergman, who make me so happy to be a Puffin author. Thanks, too, to the Philomites—Michael Green, Liza Kaplan, Brian Geffen, and Talia Benamy— whose support made the writing of this book possible. And thank you to all of my non-Penguin friends and family who listened to me talk far too often about the mechanics of kissing while wearing helmets and goggles and who traveled with and/or hosted me on research ski trips this past winter. When I follow my heart, it leads me to all of you. No question about it.

TURN THE PAGE TO FIND LOVE ON THE BEACH IN

FOLLOW *Your* HEART

summer love

YOU LEAN YOUR HEAD against the train window and watch the ocean as it whizzes by. You've listened to the summer playlist you created on your iPod twice through already, and there's still another half hour until your stop. Your cousin Tasha pokes you in the shoulder.

"Twizzler?" she asks, loud enough that you can hear her over your music. You pop an earbud out of your ear and take the candy she's offering.

"Thanks," you say, before you chomp down.

Tasha grabs one herself. "So," she says, "I never asked. Did you get everything you wanted for your birthday?"

You chew as you think about your sweet sixteen, which was six—no, seven—days ago. "The party was great," you say. "And this beach trip, just you and me, is the most awesome gift ever. But I guess there was one thing I'd been hoping for."

You sigh and take another bite of Twizzler, but Tasha won't let you off that easy.

"Which was . . . ?" she asks, raising an eyebrow.

You pull your hair over your eyes so you don't have to look at her when you say it. "I was hoping Tyler Grant was going to kiss me."

You tuck your hair back behind your ear and look at Tasha. Even though you both live in the same city, you go to different schools, and she's two years older, so she doesn't know all of your friends.

"Is that the hot ginger?" she asks. "The one who was dancing with you at the end of your party?"

You shake your head. "No. Tyler's the tall one with the hipster glasses. The one who didn't really dance much at all."

Tasha runs her Twizzler back and forth across her lips as she thinks. "Oh! The one in the green shirt! I remember him." She gives you an appraising look. "You can do way better than that."

"I don't know," you reply, finishing the last of your candy. "He's really cool. And funny—like in a sarcastic way."

Tasha puts her hand on your arm. "Trust me, cuz.

You can do better." Then her face lights up. "I have an idea! Since this is your birthday present beach weekend, you should make it your mission to get a birthday kiss from the cutest boy you can find."

"I'm not sure," you say, mostly because you're afraid you might fail at this mission, and then it would be doubly disappointing.

"How about . . . you don't have to kiss him. You can if you want, but your mission will be to flirt with the cutest boy you can find."

You smile. That sounds doable.

"Deal," you say, holding your hand out to Tasha.

"Deal," she says back, shaking it.

Then you both start laughing, and Tasha says, "I still bet you can find someone to kiss, though."

You make what you hope is a coy face, and then pop your earbud back into your ear. Secretly, you wish Tasha is right and you can find someone to kiss this weekend. But only time will tell.

✳

TWENTY minutes later, Tasha shakes your shoulder, jolting you out of a very real dream in which you were kissing Tyler Grant, and shoves your duffel bag at you. "Next stop is us! We've got to get our stuff together!"

You blink a few times, and then throw your magazines, empty smoothie cup, iPod, and sweatshirt into a tote and stand with a bag on each arm. The train slows to a stop as the conductor calls out the station name, and you follow Tasha and about a billion other people out of the train toward the beach.

The minute you get onto the train platform, Tasha is scanning the parking lot for Jade, her best friend and soon-to-be college roommate. Tasha and Jade have spent every summer together since Tasha's parents bought a beach house the year she turned eight.

You see Jade sitting in the front seat of a convertible, next to her brother Dex. But before you can point it out, Jade yells "Tash!" and then stands up on the seat. "Over here!"

You and Tasha head to Jade and Dex's car, toss your stuff in the trunk, and jump over the sides into the backseat.

"Hey," Dex says to you. "Happy birthday!"

"You, too," you answer. Dex's birthday is a day before yours—a year and a day, actually— something you learned ages ago, when you and your parents came for a visit. "Do anything fun?"

He shrugs. "You know, the usual." You don't know what "the usual" means, but you're too caught up in looking at Dex's face to ask. His hair is the same curly blond it's always been, but in the last year he seems to have grown cheekbones—and a beard. Really, it's just light blond stubble across his cheeks and chin, but it looks very manly. You think about your plan and wonder if Dex is the guy to flirt with. Maybe even kiss. Before you can decide he says, "So, where to, ladies? Want to come to the country club with Jade and me, or should I drop you somewhere else?"

Tasha looks at you. "Your choice," she says. "We can go with Dex, or we can head to my parents' place and unpack. Whatever you want."

Skip ahead to page 7 if you decide to go to the country club with Dex.

- - - - -

Skip ahead to page 13 if you'd rather head home first.

DEX looks at you through the rearview mirror with blue eyes that are so dark they're almost navy. "So?" he asks.

Even though you're still a little tired from the train trip and being woken up right before the station was called, you decide you might as well make the most of your birthday weekend. "To the country club!" you say.

Dex floors it, and Jade whoops as she takes the elastic out of her hair and lets it whip around her head. "I love the summer!" she shouts into the wind.

You lean back against the seat and let the sun soak into your skin. Dex is going too fast for you all to have a real conversation anyway.

He pulls up to the front of the country club, and a valet comes around to open the car door for you and Jade. There's another one on Tasha and Dex's side, opening their door.

"Will we have the car all afternoon?" the valet on Dex's side asks him.

"Not sure yet," Dex answers. "I'm at the ladies' beck and call today." His eyes flick over to you, and you smile. Then the four of you head inside to the dining room.

"I'm so hungry I could eat, like, six salads," Jade says.

Dex rolls his eyes. "Jade, you wouldn't be so starving if you actually ate breakfast."

"A cup of coffee totally counts as a normal breakfast, right?" Jade turns to you and Tasha.

You shrug. "I usually eat cereal," you say.

"And I usually eat yogurt," Tasha adds. "But if that's what you want to eat for breakfast, I think that's totally fine, Jade."

"See?" Jade says to Dex.

You've made it to the maître d' stand, and the four of you stop.

"Would you like a table outside or inside?" the maître d' asks.

"Absolutely outside!" Jade says, before anyone else can answer.

You can't help but smile at her summer excitement as you follow her, Tasha, and Dex to the patio. You sit down under an umbrella, overlooking the pool and the tennis courts, and very quickly there's a glass of iced tea sweating in your hand and Cobb salad sitting in front of you. Dex is next to you with his own iced tea, and a chicken sandwich on his plate. He's very involved in eating. Tasha gives you a look that very clearly means: Talk to him! And so you clear your throat and you do.

"So, um, Dex, do you have any special plans for the summer?" you ask him.

He nods as he finishes swallowing. "Well, I'm going to work in my dad's law office out here—they have a satellite office because two of the partners have summer houses nearby—and then I'm going to play as much tennis as possible."

Tennis! You'd almost forgotten how good he was at tennis. You're pretty good, too, actually, but he doesn't know that. He's never seen you play. And you've never talked about it, either, because you hate sounding braggy. "Oh right," you say, "you won the junior tennis tournament for the club last summer when I was here."

He nods, taking a sip of iced tea. "I'm hoping

for a repeat, but this time with the adult tennis tournament. They won't let me play with the kids anymore."

You laugh. "Does that mean you're officially a grown-up now?"

"Oh, absolutely," he says, with mock sincerity.

You look over at Tasha, who's listening to Jade talk about colors for their dorm room, and Tasha gives you a subtle nod. Clearly you're on the right track with this flirting business.

"So now that you're a grown-up," you say, "does that mean that you, um, read the newspaper every morning?"

"And brew my own coffee, and wear a tie to work, and walk the dog," he answers.

"You doink." Jade stops her discussion about whether hunter green and navy blue would make their dorm room feel too dark to admonish her brother. "We don't even have a dog!"

Dex laughs, and you do, too.

"Guess according to Jade I'm not quite a grown-up yet."

"Oh, little brother," Jade tells him, "even when you're ninety-nine and I'm a hundred, I'll still call you out on being a doink."

"Do you see what I have to deal with?" Dex says to you.

"Well, I don't think you're a doink," you answer. "You're not at all doink-ish to me."

Dex turns to Tasha. "Why don't you bring her around more often?"

You try not to smile too wide, but clearly you're not so bad at flirting. Just as you take another bite of your salad, three guys and three girls in tennis whites come over.

"Dex!" one of the guys says. "Any chance you're free this afternoon? Jed and Cali bailed, and we need two more for mixed doubles."

"Jade?" one of the girls says. "Any interest in playing against us with your brother?"

Jade wrinkles her nose. "The only kind of 'serve' I plan to think about today is the kind where the guy at the pool brings me lemonade while I read magazines and get tan."

"Well, I can play," Dex says, "even if my sister won't."

Tasha raises an eyebrow at you, then says, "I don't know if she's mentioned it, Dex, but that girl sitting to your right has a killer backhand."

The tennis guy who spoke to Dex first looks at

you, intrigued. "You play?" he asks.

You nod. "I'm not as good as Dex, but I'm on my school's tennis team."

Dex cocks his head at you. "How did I not know that?" he asks.

You shrug.

"Well, you want to play with us this afternoon? Did you bring tennis clothes?" He takes another sip of his iced tea.

You do have some tennis clothes in your bag in the car. . . .

"Or you can come hang by the pool with us," Jade says, "if you'd rather relax. You can always play tomorrow."

Pick up a copy of
summer love
*to continue on your journey
to find your perfect match!*

AS cute as Dex has become, you can't stop thinking about the time he peed in his pants the summer he turned seven because he didn't want to run to the bathroom in the middle of the Fourth of July fireworks. And how he once gave himself a hickey on his arm just to see if he could. And the way he used to tease you because you didn't like swimming in the ocean. There was just too much history here. Kissing Dex would be like kissing your cousin. Besides, you're feeling kind of grimy from your train ride and wouldn't mind washing your face and unpacking for the weekend before starting on your flirt hunt.

"I think maybe a trip back to the house would be best," you tell Tasha, "as long as you really don't mind."

"Not at all," she says. And then turns to Dex, "To the house, sir!"

Jade laughs. "Dex getting his license is the best thing that ever happened to me. Now I have a chauffeur to take me everywhere!"

"Hey, watch it, or I'll leave you all on the side of the road," Dex says, staring straight ahead.

"Do that, and I'm sure we'll find some cute boys to take us where we want to go, right, girls?" Jade turns around to wink at you and Tasha.

"Absolutely!" Tasha says.

> *Pick up a copy of*
> *summer love*
> *to continue on your journey*
> *to find your perfect match!*